PUFFIN BOOKS

GANGAMMA'S GHARIAL

Shalini Srinivasan likes animals, walks and nonsense. Her first novel, *Vanamala and the Cephalopod*, is a Crossword Book Award nominee and was featured in the prestigious White Ravens international catalogue.

GANGAMMA'S GHARIAL

SHALINI SRINIVASAN

Illustrations by Archana Sreenivasan

PUFFIN BOOKS

PUFFIN BOOKS

Published by the Penguin Group

Penguin Books India Pvt. Ltd, 7th Floor, Infinity Tower C, DLF Cyber City, Gurgaon 122 002, Haryana, India

Penguin Group (USA) Inc., 375 Hudson Street, New York, New York 10014, USA

Penguin Group (Canada), 90 Eglinton Avenue East, Suite 700, Toronto, Ontario, M4P 2Y3, Canada

Penguin Books Ltd, 80 Strand, London WC2R 0RL, England

Penguin Ireland, 25 St Stephen's Green, Dublin 2, Ireland (a division of Penguin Books Ltd)

Penguin Group (Australia), 707 Collins Street, Melbourne, Victoria 3008, Australia

Penguin Group (NZ), 67 Apollo Drive, Rosedale, Auckland 0632, New Zealand

Penguin Books (South Africa) (Pty) Ltd, Block D, Rosebank Office Park, 181 Jan Smuts Avenue, Parktown North, Johannesburg 2193, South Africa

Penguin Books Ltd, Registered Offices: 80 Strand, London WC2R 0RL, England

First published in Puffin by Penguin Books India 2016

Text copyright © Shalini Srinivasan 2016
Illustrations copyright © Archana Sreenivasan 2016

ISBN 9780143334071

Typeset in Minion Pro by Manipal Digital Systems, Manipal
Printed at Thomson Press India Ltd, New Delhi

A PENGUIN RANDOM HOUSE COMPANY

For Amma—lover of mountains, hoarder of plants, digger of beds, filcher of cuttings, champion composter, and knower of words like *karpuravalli*—with love

Part I

A Long Time Ago

Jayanti awoke with a horrible feeling of wrongness. As she put her feet on the floor, its smooth material pulsed lightly against them—once, twice, thrice. A sabha had been called—and she was late. She walked quickly through the long corridors of the northern yaksha palace, worrying nameless worries. The floor throbbed urgently at every step. She was needed.

Jayanti strode into the sabha and stopped. Yakshas huddled in little groups, talking busily. She walked up to the nearest group and tapped Chitrasena on the shoulder.

He turned his beady, red pigeon-y eyes upon her. It was a kind look, almost pitying. 'Jayanti!' he said.

'What's going on?' asked Jayanti.

'Your brother,' said Chitra in the sweet coo he used when truly angry. Green and purple flecks shimmered on his neck as he tilted his head to one side and eyed her. 'He and his friends have taken the lotuses Outside.'

'No!' said Jayanti.

'Yes,' said Chitra. 'All twelve of them have been contaminated beyond our wildest fears. The sabha agreed to send the guards after them. I hope you're ready . . . unless you feel you might be better staying Inside. I understand you have too many feelings in this matter. Like your brother.

3

*It must be that human form you were both born with—so
messy!'*

Jayanti's people were always wary of feelings, but few
yakshas scorned them as much as Chitra did. She stood
erect and said formally, 'I serve our people, Chitrasena. Now
excuse me please, I must gather the Winged Guard.'

As she walked away, she transformed, her body growing
taller and larger and blacker. Huge wings sprang out of her
back and she flexed them wide. 'All here?' she asked.

Murmurs came from various corners of the sabha.

'Let's go!' She rose to the roof and paused. Her people
lived in a vast palace completely sealed from the Outside.
There were no doors or windows. Their air was specially
made Inside, so it would be pure and no one could breathe
it except the yakshas themselves—they needed neither food
nor water. The more orthodox yakshas of her tribe, like
Chitra, believed that they should try to survive without
air, letting nothing in or out of their bodies. Jayanti
breathed in deeply and wondered if they were right. This
was no time for thinking, she told herself. She gathered
her magic and shifted her body through the roof, through
the layers of rock and ice that cocooned their palace, and
moved Outside.

A chilly wind hit her and she smiled with pleasure. There
was nothing quite like flying. Her people were wary of going
Outside—like breathing, it allowed one to take in too many
external things—but Jayanti always felt more alive in the air,
watching the sun glint off the ice and hearing the birds call. It
was the one thing she and Jayant agreed on . . .

'Oh no!' said Jayanti aloud, as she so often did when thinking of her stubborn, Outside-obsessed, lotus-eaten brother. What had he done now? What mess had he left for her to clear up?

It was late evening when twelve black, winged yakshas hovered low over a fresh green hill, which was surrounded by lots of other hills, each one green and minty. The sky was a deep, purply blue, heavy with rain clouds. A stream chortled down the hill and bounced into a tank, sloshing around delightedly before rushing off downhill. The tank gleamed blue and green with the hills and the sky. Its more shallow areas were pink and green with lotuses.

On the very edges grew a tangle of reeds, sticking tall, furry, brown spikes into the air. The yakshas landed among the reeds in a cloud of black wings and looked around them. The tangle of plants and muddy water below them was full of creatures—pond-skimmers and frogs, tiny fishes and reed warblers that went about their business as dragonflies patrolled above. A coot wandered in briefly, wondering if there was anything interesting to eat, before leaving the reeds for the open water where the rest of its codgery was floating around idly.

At the far edge, where the reeds were the tallest, sat a girl watching the frogs. She sat very still, her knees tucked under her chin, making it plain that she was not going to move or speak. She looked up when the twelve yakshas landed and watched with fascination while they changed, their wings swirling about their bodies as they took on new shapes. There was something both precise and fluid in the way they changed, rippling out of one shape into another like water being poured into a new glass jug. Each yaksha was now a different kind of creature—made up of bits of animals and birds and humans, even plants. They were glorious. The girl had heard stories about yakshas—how they could melt into the earth and sweep through the skies, taking any form they wished. But she had never imagined how their magic would look. It was as if the yakshas carried their own light with them, crisper and brighter and sharper than the everyday sunlight everyone else stood in.

The yakshas must have felt the girl watching for they all turned to look at her. A tall man-shaped yaksha, the most human-looking of the twelve, put his almost entirely human finger up to his almost entirely human mouth in a gesture of silence. The girl gave him a half-nod and he gave her a quarter-smile. They understood each other.

The girl noted then (for she had been too busy gawking at the way they changed and shimmered to see what they were up to) that the twelve yakshas were carrying in their thirty arm-like limbs (some had more than two and others had less) some kind of plant—as green as the hills, with long, round stalks sticking out everywhere. One, who looked mostly like a tree, had woven the stalks into its branches. Another, with a crest like a heron's and the patient, hungry air of a wading bird, jerked its head towards the tank and said, 'Here.' It was not a question, for the others quite agreed. They didn't have time to compare spots. An antlered yaksha turned to the human-looking one and said, 'This is a bit small. Maybe we could look some more? Are you sure the Winged Guard will come after us? Surely Jayanti will understand, calm them down . . . You're her brother!'

The human-shaped yaksha nodded impatiently and only said, 'She's probably leading the attack.' His face broke into an affectionate smile, as if it was an old joke between him and this Jayanti, and the others laughed with him. The heron-like yaksha walked into the tank, picking his way carefully. The others followed—the antlered yaksha going last—and slipped into the water quietly. The coots watched curiously, their white-fronted faces making them look at once absurd and mocking.

When the water reached its waist, the heron yaksha bent down into the water to feel the ground. Slowly, it felt for an empty spot among the roots of the large pink lotuses. It found one and dug a hole with one hand. Then it carefully took a lotus from its hand—the girl could see that they all held lotuses—and buried its roots in the soil. Around it, its companions did the same. Dig, bury, dig, bury. The new lotuses were indistinguishable from the pink lotuses. The man-shaped yaksha finished first. 'Hurry up!' he said impatiently, 'this is no time to be all perfect, Mahendra! Just get it over with.'

As the tree yaksha finished planting the last lotus, a flash of lightning lit up a neighbouring hill. 'The others are close,' said a woman. Her tail was spiked with scales and her teeth gleamed like a crocodile's. She gave the girl a friendly wink. The man-like one glanced up and smiled at the girl too. She noticed his eyes were glossy black, with no white showing. The yakshas patted their lotuses and walked towards the centre of the lake. As they moved deeper, the water rose over their chests, their necks, their chins, their noses and their snouts and their beaks, and over their heads. Soon, even the crests—of those who had crests—went under. Last of all, near the centre of the lake, the tree yaksha's topmost branches disappeared too.

The tank shone placid again, blue with the rain clouds, green with the hills and pink with the flowers. Glossy black-and-white coots drifted around.

The girl sat very still among the reeds. The yakshas had gone and she had lost interest in the frogs but she felt uneasy, unsafe. Something black flew above her, croaking hoarsely. It was no frog; a huge winged creature streaked across the sky, then circled back to the tank. Another came, and then another, calling out. More yakshas—and these seemed angry. The rain clouds thickened, and lowered themselves around the hill and the tank, soaking everything and bringing darkness with them. They crashed into each other. Lightning struck again and again, illuminating the hills, the trees, and the rocks one by one, as if searching for something or someone. The first twelve yakshas, the girl guessed.

The new yakshas crawled, strode and flew all over the hill. They rustled the hedges and thwacked the grasses. They shook the trees and made the rocks shudder, and they looked everywhere for the twelve drowned yakshas. The ground quaked and trembled as if the whole hill was being torn apart. Water from the tank rose and splashed against the banks. The girl was cold and wet and frightened, and somewhat nauseous from the shaking, but she didn't move. The mud under her grew warm and soft, and she sank into it gratefully. All evening and all night, she stayed still and let the mud hold her close.

In the morning, she awoke when the sky had lightened. The mud felt cold and grainy against her skirt, which had once been a lovely pink. She stood up slowly. Her legs ached with the cold and from sitting crouched over all night. Her toes seemed to have frozen into stone. She walked stiffly into the tank to rinse off the mud. As she bent, something gleamed in the water. She picked it up. It was a tiny earring in the shape of a creature, glowing with gold and jewels. It was too shiny, too glittery. She dropped it back in and concentrated on wringing out her skirt, failing to notice that the creature was opening and closing its mouth frantically, as if speaking to her, and that bubbles were coming out.

She finished rinsing her skirt just as the sun came up, making everything warmer. She splashed some water on her face and then rinsed her mouth, gargling noisily. The girl grinned and walked into the lake, into the lotuses. She wanted to see what exactly the suicidal yakshas had been planting. The new lotus plants looked just like the old ones. They had been so skilfully planted and so thoroughly smoothed over by the weight of the water that they didn't look recently dug up. She went to where she had seen the tree person bend and examined several plants. At least one of these was a new plant, she knew. But she didn't know which one. She was ready to give up, when a bud began to open. It was blue, the clean blue-purple of rain clouds. A delicious scent of cinnamon and pine filled the air. The girl felt happier, her frozen legs felt warm and energetic. She bent to sniff the flower more deeply, and she saw gooey frogspawn around the stem. The water rippled and the frogspawn twisted and waved into what might have been letters, each word giving way to a new one as she read it. And what the letters could be suspected of saying was this:

Flee. Forget this place, forget what you saw. Leave immediately.

The dot above the second maybe-i of *immediately* was an apple seed. Apples were rare in that area, but the girl's parents were traders and she had seen—and eaten—many exotic fruits, which they bought at the nearest port and transported to the king's court at Talakad. She picked up the seed. Then she reshaped the gluey spawn to say *Thank you*. She waited a moment for the next ripple to push it out of shape and then she left. Behind her, the lotus closed again. It wasn't safe either.

The girl's parents—though relatively relaxed as parents went—would be worried, she knew. She climbed down the hill, homewards.

Numb, Jayanti felt grateful for the silence Inside. She lay down wearily. She shifted her body into a turtle, tucked herself under the shell and tried to sleep. She couldn't. She had felt Jayant there—she knew she had! What had he done? Had she imagined him? Where was he? Was he dead? Why hadn't he said bye? Because he knew she would've tried to stop him—but still. He should have at least come to see her one last time. Her mind couldn't rest. She shrugged off the turtle and took the winged form again and went Outside. She flew back towards the tank where she had felt him last. There would be clues there. There had to be!

The girl's home was gone. In fact, the entire village was gone. There had been a landslide in the night; rocks and mud and scree covered everything. Only the bits of tile and wood and brick sticking out of the mud indicated where she had lived all her life.

It felt very unreal. The girl picked her way across the bits of mud and brick, trying to guess where her house had been. It was no use. The landslide had completely altered the hillside. The girl tried to find her house anyway, picking up bits of blue wood, wondering if they were from the doors of her house. After an hour, she sat down suddenly, as if all her muscles had gone on strike. Her collection of blue wood fell from her hands. She squished her knees under her chin, hugged them, and cried. She cried and cried and cried—for her mother, her father, her cat, her lizard collection, her home, and the fact that they had all gone away without her. She felt left out, abandoned.

She cried harder.

The sun was halfway up the sky when she stopped crying. She hadn't stopped entirely, of course—she wouldn't for many weeks. But she stood up. She wiped her sore eyes and looked around to see what was left.

A few villagers were huddled around a lady who was clearly a stranger. She was dressed in a beautiful silk sari with complex pleats. No one in the village tied their sari like that. Her hair was glossy and black, shining almost purple where the sun hit it. Like a crow's feathers, the girl thought. The lady had a sheaf of palm leaves upon which she was writing. The girl clutched her apple seed in her pocket and steeled herself to go up and meet the people. At the edge of the group, an older lady the girl didn't recognize looked at her blearily. 'Are you looking for your parents?'

The girl shook her head. She didn't want to think about what her parents might look like under the rubble. It was easier to think that they had just ceased to exist. More tears came at the thought.

The lady understood. She patted the girl's shoulder. 'See that lady? She has come from Talakad, from the king. She's an official at his court, it seems. If you give her your name and age, she will put you on her list. Then they'll give you a food ration and somewhere to take shelter for a few weeks till you're on your feet again. Go join the line, ma.'

The girl walked towards the line. The official was sitting under a peepal tree, one of the few things to have survived the night. She was bent over a palm leaf, writing busily. From the back of the line, the girl could hear her murmur to the man in front of her.

'And did you see any portents of this disaster? Witches? Asuras? Some kind of animal spirits? Shapeshifters?'

She didn't say the word *yaksha*.

'No,' said the man.

'They might have been in disguise. People who didn't look like people?'

'No,' said the man.

The girl looked right at the official now, at her hair and her face and her feet. She wasn't human. Oh, she looked fully human, even more than the yaksha who had first noticed her at the tank the previous night. Her fingers and toes were perfectly shaped, and there was no sign of a crest, a tail, or a claw. But her eyes were wrong. The girl knew she had to leave at once.

❧

Jayanti looked up, feeling the eyes upon her and saw a girl walking away. There was something about the girl that called to her.

'*Who's that?*' *she asked sharply.*

'*A survivor. She just lost her parents,*' *said an older lady, '*I think she lost her voice in the shock. Maybe even her memory. She was covered in mud, poor child, and sobbing her eyes out. I think she may have dug herself out of the hill. Let her have some time alone. I'll find her when it's time to eat.*'

Jayanti wanted to run after the girl. She wanted to grab
her and scream at her, 'What do you know? Where is my
brother? Tell me or I'll call lightning to strike down every
single person in what's left of your pathetic village.'

But no. What good had impulses done Jayant? Time and
patience was the yaksha way. Jayanti nodded at the old lady
and bent over her list. She kept asking questions, kept lying
about food from the king, kept collecting the names of the
dead and the living. As the day wore on, she felt more and
more ashamed of the destruction that her troops had caused,
and angrier and angrier that it had been for nothing—for
there was no sign of Jayant's body.

That night, she went back Inside, tired and unhappy.
She had found nothing. She shrank her wings and became
a crow. It reminded her of Jayant turning somersaults as he
flew. She felt cold and alone and wondered if this was how
one became perfect and ascended—frozen into stillness, too
depressed to think or feel. Jayanti tucked her head under her
wings. She forced her breathing into a slow rhythm and slept.

The girl walked away, still clutching her apple seed. She
didn't take the road, or even one of the smaller paths the
cowherds used. She walked north. She had heard that far
north, they had the kind of weather apple trees liked and
she was determined to grow her seed. She walked and
walked, avoiding all people, not staying anywhere more
than one night. She crossed rivers and hills, plateaus and

plains. She passed silently through thick forests, getting better and better at not being noticed. She walked softly past an angry king cobra, which was standing upright and tall like a warrior, its hood spread out in annoyance. It didn't see her. She snuck past a hunting tiger crouched hungrily in the grasses. It didn't smell her. She sat on a tree and watched a grumpy bear snarl at every creature who passed by, but it didn't hear her.

Eventually, she reached a range of mountains more massive than she had imagined mountains could be. Their lower slopes were covered in tall, dark pines. Their heads were stuck in the clouds and when the clouds cleared, she could see that their tips shone with snow. She started to climb their foothills. She walked more slowly now, picking her path carefully, looking for a sheltered valley she and her apple seed could live in.

She was glad to stop travelling. Her feet were covered in blisters from months of walking and, since she had no tools, her hands were soon torn and chapped and bleeding from digging the apple seed a hole.

The apple seed was snugly buried in the mud, when far to the south, the monsoon arrived at the tank. Tiny blue lotuses bloomed among the large pink ones and a delicious smell wafted through the air. The people who had remained built new houses and tilled new fields. They were beginning to feel more or less happy. They never did see

any food or money from the king. The people didn't mind, mostly because they were glad to forget the official lady. No one wanted to meet her again, for she had been angry and frustrated, shouting at everyone and demanding they tell her about the strangely shaped asuras she claimed had destroyed their town.

The people rarely talked about the landslide, except in the stories they told and the songs they sang on rainy nights as lightning slashed across the skies outside. In the stories, mysterious shapes walked across their hill. These shapes were not human but came from the skies. They had antlers and crests and long, flat flippers, others had branches and paws and delicate pink beaks. They came with the rains, and they made the tank slosh over and the fields richer and the flowers bloom. Most important of all, they were the people who brought with them the delicate blue lotuses that smelt of another world.

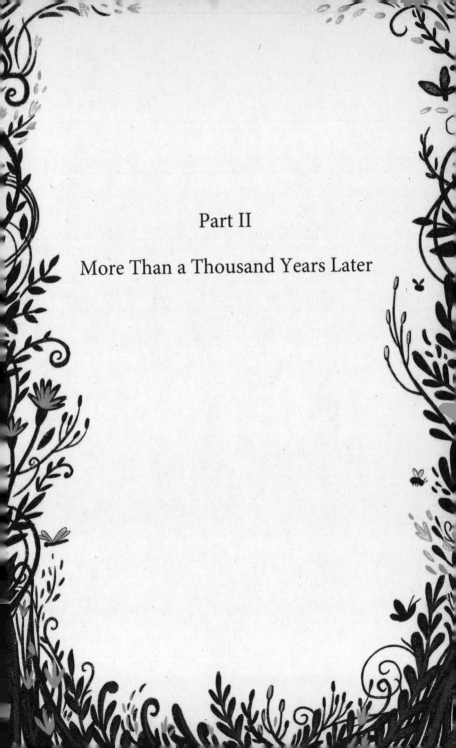

Part II

More Than a Thousand Years Later

Chapter 1

Jayanti was bored. The yearly sabha was in full swing. The northern yaksha palace—normally so quiet—rang with voices, each convinced that their path to perfection and a higher plane was the best. For centuries, the yearly sabha had left her indifferent. She didn't really believe there was a higher plane and even if there was, she didn't think that one could find it by rejecting the outside world—food, water, people, ideas, eventually even air—until one froze and hardened. But to the other yakshas, rejecting and ascending were hugely important, almost sacred. Only a few ever managed it. These yakshas would keep getting harder until they began to press in on themselves, becoming smaller and denser and blacker and hotter. Slowly, the black would turn so deep it would become clear, and still the yakshas would get smaller. At last, they would reach true perfection when their entire bodies became clear, colourless diamond that everyone could see through. Jayanti had never quite understood her people's obsession with diamonds. Their clear icy angles were too still and unmoving for her; the light glittering inside, bouncing and splitting, and gleaming off each facet merely made her miss the sun and the ice. Yakshas who managed the hard and gruelling task of turning themselves into diamond were honoured. Their statues lined the walls of the sabha, staring dully ahead of them for all eternity. In the last few centuries, no yaksha had managed to harden and freeze into diamond—though more of them tried every year. No one even managed to turn black and harden, which was the first and the easiest step, the one that could be undone. It didn't seem worth it to Jayanti. Who wanted to spend the rest of their life in the boring sabha surrounded by squabbling friends and relations? This year she felt so impatient, she wanted to scream. She suppressed a yawn.

'Still at the mercy of air, eh Jayanti?' cooed Chitrasena, his voice breaking into her thoughts and startling her. 'I'm going to speak next, you know. I posit that for true perfection, we must stop breathing. At the very least, no more visits Outside. Every time one person goes and returns, they carry in so many foreign things—skin cells and pollen and particles that contaminate us all! Our lungs are filled with impure air!'

'You took the same position last year, didn't you?' asked Jayanti politely. She was still on edge but there was no need to anger Chitrasena. He was powerful in the sabha. Oh, she had her own power as head of the Winged Guard, but yakshas are immortal, and they remember grudges for thousands of years. She had been regarded suspiciously for centuries after Jayant . . . it was only her position in the guard that made the yakshas finally accept that she had nothing to do with

that incident. That and the fact that she was one of the few yakshas who openly stood against Chitrasena's obsession with not breathing. Everyone was terrified that one day he'd just shut down the air-making rooms and let them all suffocate.

Jayanti waited silently until Chitrasena stood at the centre of the sabha and started speaking. With everyone turned towards him, she slipped away. Thinking about Jayant always made her feel like this. She needed to be Outside. She missed the joyfulness of flying—the feeling of updrafts lifting her wings, the way the earth sped under her, even the cold. It had been too long. She hesitated and then transformed. Orange feathers covered her neck and her arms grew into wide grey wings. As soon as she was fully a lammergeier, she leapt gladly into the air and shifted Outside. This was life, she thought, this was true perfection—not dully turning into diamond. She laughed in pure delight and flew south, looking for some nice mountains to fly between.

Gangamma lived in the small town of Giripuram, which was built along the sides of a small green hill set among lots of other green hills. It was a temple town, which meant that everyone in Giripuram was in some way connected with the delicately carved grey granite temple that some centuries-dead person had built. It had only one road leading from the lake, set about halfway up the hill, to the temple which was about three-quarters the way up. Above the temple, the top of the hill was a wild tangle of rocks and plants—tiny herbs and tall grasses, ferns and shrubs, all covered with flowers and berries.

People came from far, far away to see the temple. They came partly to see the twelve gardener gods and partly to wander through the fabulous bazaar that lined the last kilometre to the temple. The bazaar road was as old as the temple and paved with the same stone. It was lined with long buildings, each held up on intricately carved pillars that were covered with strange birds and animals and flowers all crowding into one another. The buildings were divided up into tiny stalls where people arranged their wares to face the road. Inside each stall were different smells, different colours. It was not unknown for pilgrims to take two hours to walk from one end of the bazaar to the temple, for there were so many things to see.

There was the attar seller with his stack of beautifully shaped glass bottles in different colours—pale pink for rose, light green for camphor, deep green for cedar, golden yellow for sandalwood, deep orange for saffron and a delicate purplish-blue for the blue lotus. On sunny days, he arranged the bottles so that the sunlight streamed through them, throwing across the shop floor glints of green and yellow and pink and pale violet. Next to him were the spice sellers, with their jars of saffron and cloves and cinnamon and nutmeg, and a persistent smell of camphor that crept into everything and wouldn't leave—people could smell it years after they had left Giripuram. Across the road from them were the weavers, laying out silk and linen and the

softest cotton, printed all over with flowers and animals that no one had ever seen.

Then there was food, all kinds of food—salted peanuts, boiled and roasted; the raw mango lady who came for exactly two weeks in the early summer with her delicious salt-and-peppered red-faced mangoes. There was the forest lady with her golden jars of wild honey and her fruit piles that changed every week—rock-like wood apple, scented rose apples, purple jamun, red karonda, several kinds of glassy-green nellikai and starfruit, and lots of nameless juicy fruits in every shape and size and colour and smell. Her chief friend and competition was the special masala-dosai man who sold his delicious dosais only at breakfast time every morning and spent the rest of the day napping in the shade and handing out salty-spicy buttermilk. Next to him was the World-Famous Kapi Shop, home to jars of beans in varying shades of dark brown—each deeper and more glossy than the next. It was also home to a noisy grinder and a smell so divine that it was said the gods up at the temple wept to smell it, for their own divinity was a paltry thing in comparison. Then there was the sweet shop which smelt of jaggery and milk and elaichi and badam; and the bajji sellers who came in the evening and filled everything with their oily onion-y smell, and oh, a million others! After the food came the puppet shop, the toy shop, the jewellers' lane, the clockmakers' lane, the pottery road and the really tiny dead-end lane where the booksellers spread their wares all over the place so that buyers had to take their shoes off outside and walk on their toes so as not to stomp on anything.

Closest to the temple were the flower shops, for it was said that the twelve gardener gods in the temple loved flowers best of all plants and that the land of Giripuram was sacred to them. The soil in Giripuram was perfect for flowers—dark red and moist. The weather was perfect too, with cool mornings, dry sunny afternoons and mild drizzly evenings round the year. Plants of all kinds loved Giripuram. The hill was dotted with an ever-changing carpet of wild flowers, each a different shape and size and smell. They were a million shades of blue and yellow and white and purple and pink. In the town itself, the gardeners of Giripuram vied with each other to produce highly bred and sophisticated flowers, crisper and more fragrant than those found anywhere else in the world. They grew cheery yellow and orange marigolds and kanakambara and saamandi, seven varieties of serene white jasmine, twelve kinds of roses and deep-golden sampige.

But none of these flowers were the reason why pilgrims thronged to Giripuram. They came to see the gods, it's true, but what they *really* wanted was to sniff the same air as the blue lotuses of Giripuram, which grew nowhere else in the world. Other places have other blue lotuses but the finicky and snooty blue lotus of Giripuram grew only in the small Giripuram tank. It was a small bluey-purply lotus with a spicy-sweet smell of cinnamon and pine. It was said that its scent could drive away any grief or sorrow—temporarily, of course, for even magical flowers can only do so much. Just three Giripuram gardeners—three people in the entire world—could grow it.

Gangamma was one of them, the oldest of the three—and in her opinion, the wisest. Gangamma was seventy-nine and a quarter years old. She had lived all her life in Giripuram, most of it in a small house on the shores of the tank. On this particular morning—as she had done every morning for more than sixty years—Gangamma woke up when it was still dark and picked roses and jasmine and marigolds from her garden. She took care to pick the best ones—they were buds almost, but not quite open. The skin on her hands was rough and torn from years of being pricked by rose bushes every morning but she held each flower delicately before putting in her basket.

Lastly, she hitched her sari up to her knees, waded a little way into the tank and picked crisp blue lotuses. Giripuram lotuses were small and didn't have too many petals. They looked a little silly, in fact, their heads bobbing on their long stems as if they were overeager to agree with anything anyone said to them. Even though she'd been doing it for decades, Gangamma felt a moment of pure pride when she saw her lotuses blooming so vigorously. She patted her plants.

'Good old lotuses,' she said. 'I'll be sure to empty my tea leaves here this evening for a nice snack for you. Best lotuses in the world!'

Then she waded back, sniffing her flowers. The morning wade back with an armful of lotuses was the happiest moment of Gangamma's day.

After a quick breakfast of idlis (Gangamma ate upma and idlis on alternate days, with dosai on the days when her friend Thimma, the masala-dosai man, felt sorry for her because she was such a boring cook) and coffee, she took her baskets—one jasmine, one rose, one marigold—and a tall bucket for the long-stemmed lotuses and walked to the bazaar. She sat down at her usual place in the bazaar, between Hanumantha, the corner bookseller who was half in the main bazaar and half in the book lane, and Kempu, her slightly younger flower-selling neighbour. She sprinkled her flowers with water (Hanumantha put his hands over his books to save them from any stray drops) and put a damp sack on them so they wouldn't wilt. Then she took up her thread and sat down to weave long chains of jasmine and roses for the rest of the day.

On this day, a richly dressed man came up to Gangamma at five in the morning. Hanumantha and Kempu weren't there yet. It was still dark and Gangamma was busy arranging the lotuses in their bucket, so she didn't see him come up.

'I want all your flowers,' he said.

Gangamma looked up and gaped. The man was wearing the most peculiar clothes. He had purple velvet shoes with long, curly tips. Yellow lilies were embroidered all over them. His turban was also purple velvet, deep and furry, and he'd stuck a beautiful white feather into it. It curled out and fell over his face, covering one eye and touching his nose. It looked ticklish but he didn't seem to notice.

His jubba or kurta or shirt or whatever it was—Gangamma's interest in clothes was restricted to which plants were used to make the dyes—was a delicate white to match his feather, spangled and glittering. It had long wide sleeves that covered his hands and hung almost to the ground. Under it, the man was wearing a lungi with wonderful checks—green and yellow and pink and purple, with the occasional electric blue stripe. But Gangamma didn't notice any of these things, for she was busy gaping at his left ear. He wore a glittering stud on it. The stud was made of gold, set with closely arranged gems, and shaped a bit like a crocodile. It was green-yellow and slender. Its nose was long and thin, with teeth sticking out. At the end of its nose was a lump. Its eyes were two extra-glinty black stones. It saw Gangamma stare at it and winked.

'Hello!' said Gangamma.

The animal stuck out a small pink tongue (glittering with rubies) at her.

Gangamma was filled with a desperate desire to wear the earring.

'Do you want it?' asked the man. 'It's quite annoying really. I'll swap it for your entire stock of flowers.'

'Really?' asked Gangamma, shocked. 'It looks expensive. All those precious stones! It must cost a fortune!'

'It's the most irritating earring I've ever had!' said the man.

Gangamma looked longingly at the earring.

'You'll be doing me a favour if you take it,' said the man, sensing she was weakening. 'A boon even!'

Gangamma couldn't resist. The animal was doing a little dance, waving its weird legs in the air. She couldn't bear to not take it. 'Okay,' she said. 'But if you ever want it back, I'll be here. Ask anyone for Gangamma and they'll show you my stall and my house.'

'Not likely!' grinned the man.

Gangamma wrapped her roses, jasmine, marigolds and lotuses in old newspaper, in four separate bouquets. She sprinkled water on them so they'd stay fresh a little longer. She put them all in one of the cane baskets so the man could take them home neatly, without squishing any flowers.

'Here!' she said. 'Put these in water as soon as you can!'

The stranger bowed and hung the basket on one arm. He unscrewed the animal from his ear. He took a small, purple velvet cushion from a pocket in his lungi (Gangamma was impressed) and put the earring on it. He held the cushion out and bowed again. 'Madam,' he said formally, 'do me the honour of accepting this gharial.'

'This what?' asked Gangamma. Giripuram had no zoo and Gangamma had never travelled away from it. Why should she when all the world travelled to Giripuram to sniff her lotuses?

'Gharial,' said the man. 'That's what this animal is. Now I must hurry away.'

He swooped away grinning broadly, the flower basket swinging on his arm but Gangamma saw nothing except the gharial.

'Hello!' said Gangamma to her new gharial. 'Hi!'

The gharial opened its mouth, but Gangamma couldn't hear anything.

'Can you hear me?' she said. 'Hello gharial! Namaskara!'

Again the gharial opened and closed its mouth as if it were talking, but no sound came out.

Maybe it was talking really softly, thought Gangamma. She held it close to her ear.

'Ow!' went Gangamma. 'Ow-wow-wow!'

For the gharial had bitten her ear lobe with its sharp diamond teeth.

She moved it away hurriedly and glared at it, holding its jaws shut between a finger and a thumb. With her other hand she rubbed her wound. The gharial winked in a friendly fashion.

Gangamma understood what she was meant to do. She unscrewed the heavy gold jimki from her left ear and put on the gharial earring instead. As she screwed it on, she could hear a small hoarse voice which seemed to speak straight into her head.

'What ho, what ho, what ho!' said the gharial. 'What adventures we shall have, you and I, O Gangamma, lady of flowers! Shall we dice in Thrace today or dance in Damascus?'

'I don't dance,' said Gangamma, 'or dice. And I definitely don't take holidays. I've never been outside Giripuram.'

'What?' shrieked the gharial. 'NO. Nonsense! No holidays it seems!' it thundered into Gangamma's ear.

'Really!' said Gangamma.

'How about ships? Do you like ships? We can sail to Byzantium!'

'No we can't,' said Gangamma. 'I have a job.'

'But you've done it!' the gharial pointed out. 'You sold all your flowers and now we have nothing to do for the rest of the day. Holidays are here! Hurrah hurray!'

For a second, Gangamma wanted to take the annoying gharial off and bury it in a hole. But only for a second.

Gangamma was shocked to find that inside her was a strange feeling, a jiggling of her knees, a tingling of her toes and a humming in her head. It was travel, and it was entirely new to her.

'How do we get there?' she asked the gharial.

'Where?' asked the gharial.

'I don't know. You pick!' she said.

'Oooooh, I like you!' sang the gharial, stretching its *ooo*s. 'I do, oh yes, I do!'

There was a swish of a tail and for the first time in more than sixty years, the bazaar at Giripuram was Gangamma-less.

Chapter 2

*J*ayanti had found the perfect mountains. They were high and cold and there were lots of air currents for her to glide around on. Glossy, black, crow-like alpine choughs flew around, looking hopefully for food. One shared her air current for a while but she didn't mind. She felt peaceful and calm. Perhaps she should forget her job in the Winged Guard. She could sneak Outside and live here forever, enjoying the winds and the sunlight. She had heard that many other yakshas from other tribes wandered the earth, swimming in the seas and entwining themselves with the forests. If she lived here, she could fly all day, every day. When she was bored she could sit on a nice crag and look down at the valley below, watching the humans and the goats gather and wander. There was something about the air here. It felt like home.

She tried speaking to the chough a couple of times, but it didn't reply—couldn't, perhaps. She tried to take its form once to talk to it. It was silent. It called when alarmed, when *hungry, when excited—but it wouldn't converse. It neither asked nor answered questions. Afraid she'd offend it, Jayanti stopped trying to talk, and they flew the whole afternoon in companionable silence.*

The air was high and thin and damp. There were huge snowy peaks, tall dark forests, and a softly spicy green smell that meant—though Gangamma didn't know this at the time—that the forest had lots of deodar trees. A deep red weasel with a creamy stripe down its front twitched its whiskers and skittered away when it saw them coming. Golden marmots fluffed into holes. An icy blue stream glimmered in a soft green meadow. Everything smelt cold and clean. Gangamma had never been so bewildered or so happy. A daft grin spread across her face and froze in place. She sat on the grass and just breathed, her mouth now wide enough to eat one of the marmots.

'I knew you'd love it!' crowed the gharial. 'Holidays are the best! And mine are the bestest!'

After a while, they walked along the river (Gangamma idly kicking pebbles, all purple and swirly blue) and came to a small town. There was a man frying salty, crunchy foods and a lady selling hot ginger tea.

Gangamma walked up to them, her stomach gurgling eagerly.

'Can I have one plate of crunchy food and one mug of tea, please?' she asked politely, smiling at them. They smiled back. 'Try the pakodas! They're the best,' said the tea lady. 'And they go well with my tea.'

'I forgot to bring any money!' said Gangamma, stricken. 'We left in such a hurry. We'll have to go back, gharial!'

'Nonsense,' said the gharial. There was a slight crunch and something fell off Gangamma's ear. She bent down to see a small diamond.

'Oh!' said Gangamma.

'Just a tooth,' said the gharial, guessing what she was thinking. 'And it'll grow back. Don't worry. Now give it to her!'

Gangamma held it out obediently to the tea lady. 'Will this do?' she asked.

The tea lady gaped. She had never seen so much money in one place.

'It's far too much,' she said. 'Give me something else.'

'It's all I have,' said Gangamma. 'If you have change, you can give it to me. Otherwise just keep it.'

'Oh!' said the tea lady. 'Change for a diamond! What a thing to ask! I don't have change for a diamond! But I'll pay for your pakodas. And I have a spare room you can stay in. It used to be my daughter's. I'll give you all your meals. And anything else you need.'

'Sounds fair,' said Gangamma.

The man gave her a plate of hot, crunchy snacks and the tea lady gave her a nice mud pot full of tea. Everything was delicious. 'Have some?' said Gangamma, holding a tiny onion-y crumb to the gharial.

'No, thanks,' it said.

'If I hold the cup to my ear, will you drink some tea?' she asked, feeling slightly guilty at not being able to share her delicious holiday food with the one who brought her there.

'Please don't try!' said the gharial with a slightly nasty cackle. 'You look ridiculous enough holding crumbs to your ears. Of course if you *like* spilling tea into your ears, don't let me stop you . . .'

'Fine, I'll eat everything!' said Gangamma defiantly.

The tea lady's name was Hansa. After tea, she showed Gangamma the spare room—it had long glass windows, and a polished wooden floor that smelt of deodar. Hansa gave Gangamma a huge yellow sweater, a red monkey cap, warm black boots and green mittens. Gangamma put them all on and hurried outside.

She felt bouncy and energetic, almost as if she were thirty again. She walked up and down the hills, took off her mittens and boots and paddled in the icy river till her toes went numb. She walked through the snow and bounded up rocks. Then she ate every scrap of the massive dinner Hansa made (the gharial pointed out that metal people don't need food) and went straight to bed, burying herself under a quilt, two blankets and a shawl.

The next morning, Gangamma woke up at four, as she always did. The sky outside her window was—she was puzzled—deep black. She tried to get up and got her second shock of the morning—her joints were frozen stiff.

'Aaaargh!' she yelled.

She tried getting up again, flexing her toes extra hard and bending her knees to try and move out from under her layers of blankets. She moved about half an inch. It took her five minutes to rub and coax her legs into moving (and it didn't help that her fingers were also stiff). At breakfast, Hansa gave Gangamma cups and cups of hot tea (Gangamma tried not to miss her usual morning coffee). She noticed that Gangamma's legs were a bit wobbly and gave her a stout walking stick.

'There's a beautiful old fort up there,' she said to Gangamma, showing her some ruins halfway up a mountain. 'You should walk up there today. The view is spectacular!'

Gangamma's knees creaked in protest but Hansa was very persuasive. 'I don't want you to get bored!' she said. 'You're on holiday! You must see our beautiful land.'

'That only!' the gharial boomed in her ear. 'Go have fun. I insist!'

So Gangamma smiled politely and, leaning heavily on her stick, staggered off the chair and stood up.

'Oh, you will love that fort! Whattay fort I say! A fort for the ages. I can't wait to see how much you'll love it,' said the gharial.

'I will,' said Gangamma, bravely stuffing her swollen feet into the black boots Hansa had given her.

'Nothing to worry about, but you should leave me behind,' said the gharial.

'But—' said Gangamma.

'Gharials are cold-blooded. This place is just too cold for me. I'm going spend all day basking in the sun and getting as much heat as I can,' it said.

'But . . .' tried Gangamma again, weakly.

'You don't want me to get frostbite, do you?' said the gharial. 'What if my toes start to rot and have to be amputated?'

'What about *my* toes?' wondered Gangamma. But she was too kind to disappoint Hansa and the gharial. Off she went, ignoring her knees, her thighs, and her ankles, and hoping her nose wouldn't fall right off—fully determined to have a good holiday.

It was a lovely mountain. That much was clear. On its lower slopes were apple orchards, the trees fluffy and pink with flowers. Wisps of mist wandered around in a friendly fashion. Gangamma walked up to the nearest tree to get a better look at the flowers. They were the palest pink and the pinkest white with cheery yellow centres. She put a hand out to touch the tree trunk and bees buzzed around possessively.

'Oy!' shouted someone. 'This is private property.' It was a girl, maybe twelve years old—it was hard to tell how much person there was under her giant clothes. She was wearing a long, thick blue sweater that reached her knees. Under it were a pink skirt and huge blue boots. She was holding a large stick. On her head sat a black bird with a bright yellow beak and bright red feet. (It was an alpine chough, pronounced to rhyme with puff, but Gangamma didn't find that out till much later.)

'Croweee!' said the bird.

'What tree is this?' asked Gangamma, filled with the fierce and desperate greed of the true gardener. She wanted that tree and she wanted it now now now. And she wanted it in her garden, not someone else's. But how?

'Apple,' said the girl scornfully. 'Don't you know anything about plants? Now shove off, old lady!'

Gangamma said nothing. She didn't have the heart to climb up to the fort. But she wasn't done with the apple trees. Not yet. Terrible plans filled her mind as she strode back to Hansa's house in a hurry.

Though they still hadn't exchanged a word, Jayanti was beginning to like the chough and she thought he liked her too. He seemed to her so much a part of the quiet, cool homeliness of the valley. They were sharing an air current again that day, when the chough screamed and flew straight down.

'You're back early!' said Hansa, who was sitting cosily on her doorstep and basking in the sun.

'Whose trees are those?' asked Gangamma, pointing to the hill behind her.

'Some big shots',' shrugged Hansa.

'Will they sell me one?' asked Gangamma.

'But you're from South!' said Hansa. 'Apple trees don't grow in South. It's simply not cold enough.'

'I suppose you're right,' said Gangamma, though inside she was certain Hansa was wrong. 'I'm taking the gharial to see them.' She picked it off its warm windowsill and put it on. Waving to Hansa, she walked out fast.

'Go after lunch, na? What's the hurry?' called Hansa.

'Cold! Halp! Froze-a-croc!' shouted the gharial when the chill outside air hit it.

Gangamma ignored them both and walked on as rapidly as she could, concentrating on the hill and the tree.

Up, up, up she went, stumbling and skidding, her eyes focussed on the orchards above. Her knees creaked, her ankles kept turning in, her toes kept stubbing themselves against stones. Gangamma ignored them completely, her mind wholly absorbed by her need to get to the apple trees. The gharial seemed to feel that the earring's screw wasn't sufficiently safe and clung to her ear with its jet claws.

'Aaah!' breathed Gangamma, stopping at last. The orchard was fabulously empty. There was no sign of the girl. She wandered among the trees sniffing and admiring, not noticing a black bird floating in the air currents high above her. Gangamma came back to the first tree she had touched, at the very edge of the orchard. Though it was quite a slender tree, it looked old. Its limbs were twisty and its bark was rough and cracked.

'This one,' she said.

'This one what?' said the gharial uneasily.

'I want this one,' said Gangamma.

'Well, you can't have it,' said the girl, appearing again.

'Kweeee!' said the chough, swooping down, sticking its claws into Gangamma's bun.

'Didn't we chuck you out once already?' said the girl.

In Gangamma's head, her old respectable self was begging her to apologize, say a few polite things and leave. But Holiday Gangamma was a far bolder person. She launched herself at the tree and hugged it hard. 'Home, gharial! Take us home!' she cried.

'What the . . .! Grab them!' shouted the girl, leaping at her.

'Kweeeeeeeeeeeeeee!' screamed the bird.

Everything blurred and everyone clutched everyone and SPERR-LASH! Gangamma, the apple tree, the girl, the bird and the gharial all found themselves under water.

Chapter 3

Jayanti watched the chough swoop down towards a vaguely familiar-looking human girl, and then towards an old human woman. As she watched, the old human hugged a tree and then they were all gone. No tree, no old lady, no girl, no chough. It had to be magic. Jayanti was troubled. The mountains no longer felt home-like and friendly. And there was something about the girl that itched and tugged at her memory. What was she forgetting?

Gangamma's head shot out of the water. She sneezed and water dribbled out of her nose. She coughed and spat out a couple of weeds (some kind of water fern and a long frond of duckweed). Her mouth tasted nasty, a bitter combination of mud and weeds.

'Vlaaaargh,' she spat, sticking her tongue out.

'Cree-er,' said the bird. It seemed to have swum to land. It was sitting on the bank all wet and bedraggled, feathers sticking out in all directions.

'Blergh,' said a voice near her. It was the apple tree's girl. She looked furious.

'Better rescue her, huh?' said the gharial in Gangamma's ear.

Gangamma stretched out a hand. The girl smacked it away. Hard.

'Get the tree out! Fast!' she screamed.

Without a thought, Gangamma dived back in. She hugged the tree's grey trunk and tried to lift it up. It had settled comfortably on the mud at the bottom of the tank, and seemed to resent being moved. Gangamma yanked and pulled but it wouldn't budge. Air bubbled out of her nostrils and she knew she should move, but she didn't seem to be able to stop hugging the tree.

'Push!' said the girl, and Gangamma saw that she had one end of the tree and was pulling it towards the shore.

'Blub?' said Gangamma, releasing some more air and pushing with all her strength. In a daze, she watched the tree spin around a bit before it started to rise. It was slippery and reluctant but she and the girl managed to bring it to the shore. Once they were out of the water, the tree was heavier but Gangamma felt stronger and less unreal. She and the girl half-dragged and half-rolled it up the slope and into the garden. 'That'll do,' said the gharial, and Gangamma and the tree and the girl flopped splat in her garden, dripping pond water. The tree seemed to cheer up but Gangamma didn't notice. She had fainted.

When Gangamma awoke, she was lying on some flattened jasmine bushes. Blue-sleeved hands were gently moving the apple tree off her left arm. She rolled over a little to watch as the girl moved the tree away. The girl made unerringly for Gangamma's toolshed. She came out with Gangamma's largest digger, its top a wicked-looking spike of iron, almost as tall as she was. The girl looked around and, deciding on a spot, began to dig. She dug with sharp, controlled strokes, throwing mud out behind her in a beautifully precise arc.

Gangamma was impressed. She regarded digging as an unappreciated art. 'Too many young gardeners don't care these days,' she frequently grumbled to her friend Kempu who, at sixty, was Ganagamma's idea of a young person. Kempu laughed, continued to dig haphazardly and grow beautiful plump-looking marigolds. But not this girl. She dug with the precision of a jeweller.

'What's your name?' Gangamma called to her. Her voice, when it came out, was weak and a bit crackly.

The girl gave her a thoughtful glance that made her look suddenly old. Then she shrugged. 'Doesn't matter.'

'No, really. You're not a bad digger!' said Gangamma. This was her idea of a tremendous compliment.

The girl just looked at her. Something flickered in her face, a swift grin, but it was gone so fast that Gangamma decided she had imagined it.

'Really!' said Gangamma, unable to understand why the girl wasn't more pleased to be praised.

The girl went back to her digging. Gangamma wanted to ignore her back but she was fascinated by her. She sat up so she could watch more closely.

'What's your bird's name?' she tried again.

'It's a chough,' said the girl. 'So that's what I call it.'

'I like its feet and beak,' said Gangamma. 'Good marigold colours.' She felt pleased with herself for thinking up such a good compliment.

The girl gave her a half-grin and continued to dig. When she had a nice deep hole, the girl came back near Gangamma. She picked up the apple tree and carried it to the hole. Gangamma remembered how heavy it had felt to her in the water, and sighed. She'd've loved to be so strong. She hadn't been that strong since she was forty—if ever.

The girl set the tree in the hole. She held it straight and piled mud around it. She put in lots of dead leaves and twigs. Finally, she patted the mound into place and there stood the only apple tree in Giripuram, blooming pinky-white among the jasmine and the roses. The girl stood next to it, her hand on its trunk, and smiled. Gangamma gave a sigh of pure pleasure. She smiled at the girl, a smile of shared joy.

'That's good work,' she said. 'What's your name, ma?'

The girl looked at her for a moment. Her smile snapped shut and her mouth firmed into a decision. She took a deep breath.

'Thief! Murderer!' shouted the girl. Her voice boomed across the tank and the garden and Gangamma could only be glad all her neighbours were at the bazaar and too far to hear.

Gangamma was so used to thinking of herself as a quiet old gardener that she simply hadn't considered that she might have behaved in a most heinous fashion. She

imagined what she'd say of a person who tried to uproot and kidnap her lotuses, and her face crumpled. It was already quite wrinkled but now it collapsed into itself like an old paper bag.

'Oh!' she said. 'I am. I really am!'

'Yes,' said the girl stoutly, unimpressed by Gangamma's epiphany. 'You are.'

It occurred to Gangamma that she had kidnapped a person in addition to a tree. The girl probably had parents somewhere. Maybe a school? A teacher of some kind? They would all be worried. She grabbed the girl and the tree, one in each hand, and said aloud, 'Take us back.'

'Can't,' said the gharial. 'Oh, didn't I tell you? I can transport you to a place only once.'

'Take us back!' wailed Gangamma again.

'Really can't,' said the gharial.

The girl twisted her arm away from Gangamma and glared even more fiercely.

'Who are you talking to?' she said dangerously.

'My earring,' mumbled Gangamma.

The girl backed away from her, still glaring. 'You talk to your earring? What is wrong with you? Are you mad? Senile? Can I please speak to someone else? Your children?'

Gangamma was also beginning to wonder if she was losing her mind. 'I don't have any children,' she said.

'Spouse? Nurse? Lawyer? Anyone at all who is responsible for you?'

Gangamma shook her head.

'Next of kin?'

'No,' said Gangamma. The girl lifted an eyebrow and Gangamma felt an old worry come back. 'As a grower of the Giripuram lotus, I am supposed to train my successor,' she explained, hating herself for feeling obliged to explain to some random child. 'But I've never found anyone the lotuses and I both liked. Ragini was kind and funny and I would have adopted her if I could but every lotus she touched died. Even the roses she pruned would stop flowering. Kallu was pretty good—his mulching was spectacular—but what a dreadful boy he was! Forever pestering someone. His favourite victim was Somaiah's bull. He used to come running back home with the bull after him. He'd lock himself in the house and the bull would attack my garden instead, stomping and goring all my flowers. Then there was—'

'No one,' said the girl flatly. 'You have no one.'

'Creeeee,' said the bird.

'Me,' sang the gharial in a soft gurgle and though it could not take the girl back home, Gangamma felt happier.

'No,' she said defiantly and glared back at the girl. 'I don't mind. In fact, I like having no one.'

'Me too,' said the girl and grinned suddenly.

It was a wonderful grin, as if a warm winter afternoon had snuck into the garden. Gangamma thought she could feel the plants perking up. 'You still haven't told me your name,' she said. 'I'm Gangamma.'

'I can't tell you,' said the girl. 'Sorry,' she added kindly and again Gangamma felt like she was the child in the conversation, 'I really can't.'

'What shall we do with you then?' asked Gangamma. She felt tired and her head was still a bit woolly from fainting. She wished the girl wasn't so calm and self-possessed about being kidnapped. If only she had cried, Gangamma could've soothed her with flowers or a story, and promised to take her home. She looked helplessly at the girl.

'Were those your blue lotuses that made the lake smell so good? Can we go see them?' asked the girl.

Gangamma took off her woollens and her boots. She hitched up her sari and tied it securely at her knees. The girl watched her warily and then took off her own sweater and boots. Under it she was wearing some kind of greenish khaki blouse. The bird seemed to approve because it made a soft caw and flew away. 'Gone to explore,' the girl said to Gangamma. 'I don't think it'll be back for a few days.'

Gangamma nodded in what she hoped was a wise way. The girl's eyes narrowed.

'That's an interesting earring,' she said. 'Where did you find it?'

Gangamma told her about the man. 'And where did *he* find it?' asked the girl.

'I didn't ask,' said Gangamma. 'I just felt like I had to have it. It seemed to . . . speak to me.'

'I don't seem, I DO speak,' said the gharial loudly.

Gangamma looked uneasily to see if the girl heard. She was still frowning at the earring. 'They do, don't they?' she said softly.

'Who does?' said Gangamma a bit sharply. 'Have you seen it before?'

'What? No, I meant animals in general,' said the girl. 'I was thinking of my chough. But even the apple tree seemed to speak to me. I saw the seed and I knew.'

Gangamma nodded. From her left ear, the gharial grinned toothily. It lifted a claw to cover its eyes and mouthed, 'She can't see me!' pointing the other claw at Gangamma. It winked at the girl.

The girl ignored it and looked straight at Gangamma. 'Shall we go?' she said.

They waded carefully out into the lake, past the rushes that grew in the less shallow areas, past the floating duckweeds and into the lotuses. Gangamma patted a lotus and turned to the girl. 'This is the Giripuram lotus. Lotuses, meet Apple Girl.' The girl put out a hand and touched a lotus gently. She patted it. Gangamma was impressed to note that she was not too besotted with the flowers to appreciate the glossy, green leaves with their bluey-purple veins. She even sniffed a stem and stroked the tiny hairs that grew on it. They were too tiny to see but were velvety to the touch.

Suddenly—it was a day of suddenness for Gangamma—she said, 'Do you want to be my apprentice?'

'Okay,' said the girl absently, still looking at a leaf.

'Take today off and we'll start tomorrow,' said Gangamma.

'Can I explore the hills?' asked the girl.

'Whatever you want,' said Gangamma. 'I do not interfere with your days off. If you want a mother, find a different guru.'

'That's good,' said the girl. 'I like that. I'll be off then!' She gave Gangamma a slight grin and waded out of the tank. She put on her boots and then, without saying goodbye, set off towards the hills. The chough swooped down at her with a joyful yell and flew up again into the hills. The girl followed it.

Gangamma spent the day doing housework. She never liked it but she realized, with the eyes of someone who has been away, that her house was a mess. And had been so for at least twenty years.

She began by clearing out the old upstairs bedroom for the girl. When she had been apprenticed to her aunt, she and her aunt's daughter Meena had shared that room. Gangamma had been miserable, for she was the apprentice, there to work, while Meena was the adored daughter. Meena had been miserable too, because she thought the room and the house and the lotuses were hers. She had been furious and shocked to learn that they were never hers—and worse, that when her mother died, they would belong to quiet, permanently-muddy and sweaty Gangamma. Gangamma knew she was the most paavam person in the house; Meena was certain she was the most miserable. And as long as they lived in the same house, they had both made sure that the other person felt just as horrible as they did.

Gangamma hated that room. She never set foot in it if she could help it, and it was covered in almost fifty years' worth of dust and cobwebs. She entered it stiffly now and used a long, stiff broom to jab at the cobwebs. She dusted everything. Then she swept and swabbed the floor viciously.

After that she cleaned out the downstairs. When she was done the house was . . . well, it was all right. It wasn't homey and cosy like Hansa's but it was terribly clean. And it was *her* home. Gangamma walked to the bazaar. She sidled past the gardeners and found her friend Thimma— he could always be relied upon to have some nice food and she could tell him about her holiday.

Gangamma returned home about seven in the evening, which was her usual dinner time. Thimma had kindly given her dosais for her dinner and the girl's, rolled up neatly in banana leaves. She wandered in to find that her nice just-cleaned house was full of junk.

'What is this?' shouted Gangamma.

The girl came running in from the garden.

'I just cleaned the house! Why are all my shiny tumblers all over the windowsills? And why are they full of twigs and dead leaves?' asked Gangamma.

'They're wild flowers I found in the hills today. They're beautiful!' said the girl indignantly.

'Not right now,' said Gangamma.

She had a point, the girl had to admit. The tiny pale pink and blue flowers that looked so fragile and lovely on the hill had shrivelled into crumpled brown blotches. The large yellow lilies had gone a nasty brown and now flopped off their stems like burst balloons. The feathered ferns had shed tiny needle-like leaves all over the house.

'It's like having a green cat,' grumbled Gangamma. 'Shedding all over everything! I know it's your day off but you made this mess. You have to clean it.'

The girl sullenly swept up everything.

At dinner, for the first time, the girl showed real enthusiasm. She attacked her dosais violently and shoved huge chunks into her mouth.

'These are dosais,' Gangamma said kindly. 'Do you like them?'

The girl gave her a strange look. She hesitated for a moment. Then she grinned and said, 'Yes! So crunchy!'

As they were washing up after dinner, the girl brought up the wild flowers again. 'You like flowers! Why are you so cruel about these?'

'They're fine on the plant,' said Gangamma. 'But they're useless to pick. They die immediately.'

'Not all of them!' said the girl.

'Not one flower you brought survived,' said Gangamma.

'But there are others. The hills are full of flowers in every colour and shape and size. You have to try growing them too, not keep producing stupid marigolds.'

'And what's wrong with marigolds?' said Gangamma. She was angry now, even though she didn't really like marigolds. She thought they flowered too easily and too profusely. It made her suspicious.

'They're so boring!' said the girl. 'Where's the challenge? They just grow and grow. They grow them in the North, you grow them here. What kind of gardener gods want marigolds anyway? If I had magical powers

I'd want something more exciting. Why don't you grow different things?'

'You are an apprentice. When . . . IF you ever become a proper gardener, you can grow as many weeds as you want. I will be peacefully dead by then and won't stop you. But until then, you will learn to grow what I am teaching you to grow.'

'Huh!' said the girl rudely. 'As if you need to *teach* anyone to grow marigolds.'

Gangamma was annoyed to find that she agreed exactly with the bratty child. She decided it was best to be dignified and not argue. 'Now go to bed. We have work to do tomorrow,' she said loftily.

The story of Gangamma's strange appearance and disappearance was soon all over Hansa's town. Hansa found that, in addition to the diamond, she had gained a lot of respect from people who wanted to know every detail about the mighty enchantress who had come to their town, stolen a tree, that weird yaksha child and a chough, and disappeared into the air.

Business was wonderful. People kept visiting her tea stall to ask admiring questions like, 'So that powerful enchantress is wearing a sweater you made?'

And Hansa would laugh and say airily, 'She said it was very warm! And it's not even one of my good sweaters, you know! In fact, my daughter refused to wear it because she said it was too lumpy . . .'

And she would say it as loudly as she could so everyone in her town could hear that her least favourite sweater was still good enough to be admired by an enchantress.

'What did the enchantress want?' asked the pakoda man.

'Some yaksha business. Best not to know,' said another man. 'Everyone knows that the tree and the child and the chough were older than our village. And the child never spoke to any of us. So arrogant! Just because she was immortal! Good riddance, I say!'

If the man had looked up then, he would've seen a curious thing. High above Hansa's stall, a large bird appeared to be listening very hard to what he had to say. It was a lammergeier, a huge vulture with sharp eyes, an orange neck and legs covered in shaggy, pyjama-like feathers. It floated languidly on a nice slow updraft, keeping an eye and an ear out for anything interesting. At the man's words, its body changed smoothly, getting larger and darker. Its wings turned leathery; they flapped on, not changing their beat.

A sudden idea had come to Jayanti, so sharply that it felt utterly true. She was filled with joy and terror. Her mind screamed and whirled. Jayant! Was it really him? The chough was Jayant! Jayant was a chough! Her lawless, abandoning, possibly insane, probably part-dead brother was now a bird! Jayanti didn't know whether to be happy or frightened. One thought rose above the whirl and came to her clearly—she

hadn't even recognized him! For a moment, Jayanti wanted to scream. She breathed in deeply, letting the chill, thin air cool her mind. She felt a bit calmer. What had he done to himself a thousand years ago? Had he been twisted into some kind of monster? What was she to do with him? If it was truly him. Jayanti wavered for a moment. She knew where her duty lay but she also knew where she wanted to be. She looked first north and then south and then turned south. To Jayant. Was she being foolish? She paused, hovering, unable to decide what to do. Already some of her first glad certainty had faded, and she was beginning to doubt if it was really Jayant. She wondered if she had imagined that the chough swooped and flew and just plain felt like her brother. She waved a wing and clouds gathered towards her. She murmured to them and then swerved sharply. She flapped her enormous wings and flew straight north. Behind her, the clouds scattered. They drifted away casually, some going east, some west. But the largest, darkest clouds swept straight south.

Chapter 4

Gangamma had a strict routine for apprentices—it was the routine her aunt had made her follow as an apprentice sixty-odd years ago and she had never felt the need to change it. Apprentices had to be up early and help with the flower picking. Then, while Gangamma went to the bazaar, the apprentice had to weed and mulch and water and talk to the plants. There were always lots of little things to be done—compost pits to stir, hedges to trim, bushes to prune, cane baskets to weave and dinner to cook.

The next morning, the girl was up well before Gangamma. She had picked the lotuses and was halfway through the roses when Gangamma went into the garden. She was conscious of a slight anger—for nearly fifty years now, picking the lotuses had been the high point of her morning. But she kept quiet and watched the girl cut flowers. She held plants with a light, firm hand, so nothing got crushed or torn. She cut stems cleanly. And she was very, very quick.

'You can spend the morning weeding the jasmine bed,' said Gangamma after breakfast. This might sound harsh but weeding the jasmine bed was Gangamma's idea of a treat. Unlike the roses, the jasmines had no thorns; unlike the lotuses, they were on dry land. They grew on large wooden scaffolds at eye level, so weeding under them was shady and pleasant. The girl seemed to recognize that Gangamma was trying to be nice. She smiled and nodded and set to work immediately.

When Gangamma came back from the bazaar at lunch time, she did something her other apprentices had sworn she wasn't capable of—she hugged the girl. Never had she seen such a beautifully weed-free plot. On one side, neatly chopped and waiting to be put into the compost was a massive pile of weeds—Giripuram's lovely mud and weather were as attractive to weeds as they were to other plants. The girl had even uprooted the nasty touch-me-nots that covered the ground. Their purple stems were studded with thorns that meant anyone who pulled them out of the ground paid for it in a thousand tiny cuts.

The girl grinned. 'Neat, huh?'

'Neatest! If you won't tell me your name, I am going to call you Ondu.'

'Why?' asked the girl.

'Ondu means one. You're my number one apprentice,' said Gangamma.

'I like that,' she beamed. 'Definitely better than the name my parents gave me. I'm pleased to be Ondu.'

She laughed, and again Gangamma wondered if she was imagining that the jasmine looked crisper and more fragrant.

The next several days were among the happiest Gangamma could remember. She and Ondu worked with zeal, spending every minute they could either in the garden or talking about it. In the mornings, Ondu clambered across the surrounding hills. Gangamma went to the bazaar and sold her flowers, boasting to anyone who'd listen about her new apprentice, her apple tree, her bird and her general enthusiasm for getting muddy and sweaty. In the afternoons Gangamma came back home, and she and Ondu got to work. They dug, they weeded, they mulched, they composted. They argued about the rival merits of chicken dung and cow dung. They would have watered if they could but they didn't need to because it rained a little every afternoon, leaving everything glistening and fresh. Gangamma was soon sure that Ondu was not going to kill any of her plants. Everything she touched seemed to get crisper and smell a little better.

At the end of the week, Gangamma realized that there was nothing left to do in the garden. 'Do you want to come to the bazaar with me?' she asked Ondu.

'What's the bazaar like?' asked Ondu.

Gangamma was taken aback. She had never met anyone who didn't know all about the Giripuram bazaar. Maybe they didn't have bazaars in North, she thought. She tried to explain and soon gave up, saying only: 'It's full of food and flowers and people come from far away to see them.'

'Okay. . .' said Ondu cautiously.

'You will see lots of other gardeners there. There's my friend Kempu and there're Sesha and Sachi who are magic with sampige. I often wonder if there's some yaksha blood in them. Don't tell anyone but I sometimes think their sampige is better than the lotuses. Oh, and there's also my cousin Meena. She fancies herself a gardener but has never been quite good enough to grow blue lotuses, so she likes to snipe at me when she can.'

'What does she say?' asked Ondu.

'The usual—I'm so hideous no one married me; I'm so mean all my apprentices flee; I'm so obsessed with plants all humans are bored by me . . . that kind of thing.'

'I don't like her,' said Ondu.

'Don't worry, she won't like you either,' said Gangamma. 'She always hates my apprentices till they leave. Then she loves them.'

And so off they went. The bazaar was still quiet and sleepy when they arrived. Gangamma sat down in her usual spot next to Kempu and said proudly, 'Kempu, this is my assistant, Ondu.'

Ondu gave him a slight smile.

'So *you* are the mythical assistant, hahaha,' said Kempu. 'I hear you have the greenest thumbs in all of Asia! Like rich compost covered with bright moss after a rain!'

'Yes, very,' said Gangamma drily. 'Ondu, this is Kempu.'

'Where is your bird? I hear you have a bird? Is it shy like you? Hahahaa,' said Kempu, chuckling happily. Gangamma frowned a little. She had forgotten how annoying Kempu was until you knew him well enough to like him despite it.

Ondu said nothing. She didn't seem to have heard of politeness, Gangamma thought irritably, wishing she could leave them both there and go somewhere more peaceful.

'Picked her for her quietness-aa?' said Kempu. 'Good, good. My Kamaraj would talk the petals off a sunflower! Here he comes now. Oy, Kamesh! Come meet your new colleague.'

Gangamma tensed slightly. Kamaraj had wanted to be her assistant some years ago. She had set him to dig a compost heap and rejected him immediately for, she had said nastily, 'treating my spade like a spoon!' He had gone away swearing revenge, and she had been quite upset with Kempu for taking him on. For months afterwards, Kamaraj and Gangamma had been stand-offish and polite with each other while Kempu made horrible jokes he thought were breaking the tension, but were really making it much much worse. These days Kamaraj was quite polite, but Gangamma—who took six months to realize how rude she had been and another month to realize it was too late to apologize, and that even if it wasn't, she didn't know how to—still felt vaguely wrong and awkward around him. Kempu never noticed, but Ondu spotted her discomfort at once and stiffened in sympathy.

'Hello,' said Kamaraj politely. He gave Ondu a small smile, the perfect width to show a willingness to be friendly but not toothy enough to be actually friendly. 'If you want,

I can show you the shops during our mid-morning tiffin break.'

'Hello. Okay,' said Ondu, still not smiling.

And that was the most pleasant part of the morning.

By six, the sky had turned pale and devotees had started showing up. Food arrived with them, so they could stuff their faces before going to see the gods. The street began to smell of delicious things. Kempu and Kamaraj and Gangamma sniffed happily but Ondu was unimpressed.

'What is this horrid smell?' she asked Gangamma.

Unfortunately, she said it just as Thimma—who had heard that his friend Gangamma had brought her new apprentice to the bazaar—came by with a plate of crunchy masala dosais for them. His face fell, for it was he who had invented the masala dosais, only ten years ago. They had become instantly popular and now people made them all across the plateau and all the way to the sea. He was very proud of his masala dosais! And everyone in Giripuram was just as proud of him, for who would have thought of putting potatoes in a dosai but a true genius? Many of them privately thought that the real reason people came to Giripuram was not the lotuses or the gods but the masala dosai. Ondu didn't seem to notice that she had upset Thimma, or even that he was a friend of Gangamma's.

'It does smell gross,' she said. 'All potato-ey. Who puts potatoes in a dosai?'

'That's the point!' said Kamaraj, outraged. 'That's why it's delicious.'

'Tell her!' hissed Kempu to Gangamma. 'This is nonsense!'

'She's from North, Thimma,' said Gangamma soothingly. 'They eat different food there. She doesn't know.' A small part of her remembered Ondu crunching the dosais at dinner and she knew that being from North was no excuse.

'Hmmm,' said Thimma. But he stopped glaring.

'She'll need a couple of weeks to get used to our food,' nodded Kempu, but the glance he threw Ondu was not friendly at all. Gangamma sighed. If Kempu had stopped trying to be funny, he was *really* upset. Kamaraj, too, was eyeing her in a slightly suspicious way.

'She's adjusting slowly,' said Gangamma. 'And she's done some wonderful work in the garden.'

Thimma looked happier and Gangamma was so relieved that she just continued to gush. Her voice rose to a shout as she ended, '. . . and I've never seen anyone weed like her! And her composting is absolutely no-questions-asked perfect!'

Gangamma had overdone it. As soon as the words were out of her mouth, she wished she hadn't said them. The entire gardener community glared back at her. Colleagues, ex-apprentices, friends, rivals, seed-dealers, tool-suppliers, her least-favourite cousin Meena—every single person there thought of themselves as the best weeder and composter and every single one of them was now offended.

'Really?' beamed Ondu, not noticing the air of awkwardness.

'She's only been here a week! How do you know what her compost will be like? You can't tell!' said Kamaraj, looking hurt.

'I *can* tell,' said Gangamma quietly. 'It's a knack. You'll pick it up by the time you're as old as I am.'

'Oho,' said a lady from four stalls away, who looked a lot like Gangamma but better cared for. Ondu stared at her. Her hair was sleekly combed and pinned up and she had arranged a neat jasmine chain around her perfectly round bun. Her sari was clean and its pleats were sharp with starch. Her face was rounder and cleaner and pinkish, where Gangamma's face was usually buried beneath layers of sweat and mud, and had the crumpled, dusty look of a not-very-favourite hanky that has been turned into a rag. The lady stared right back at Ondu. A jewelled lotus-shaped stud glittered on her nose. 'I see our snooty Gangamma has finally found someone she approves of!'

'Ondu's certainly better than you!' said Gangamma stoutly.

'What do you know about her? Nothing! Where's she from? Who are her parents? She doesn't even have a real name! When you're found in a ditch with your throat slit and your lotuses kidnapped . . . well, you'll be too dead to admit you were wrong,' cried Meena. 'Better than me it seems! Pah!'

Ondu had gone pale and worried.

Gangamma eyed Meena in annoyance. 'Her compost is still better than yours,' she said coolly.

'Better than Meena is one thing. Better than us?' asked Sesha, the sampige king, who was busily threading his golden-yellow flowers into long fragrant chains. His wife, Sachi, winked at Gangamma.

Gangamma considered. She really liked Sesha and Sachi. Their garden was neat and orderly, their mud was a rich, deep red and not too clayey. Their compost was a pleasant black. But their pit was a little too soggy for her taste. She couldn't lie.

'A little better,' she said. 'She keeps the pit drier.'

Sachi turned away from her and rolled her eyes at the bazaar at large. Sesha just looked miserable.

'Who said you could judge anyone's compost? Your compost is as dry as a desert!' shouted Meena.

'And so is your head!' shouted a voice from further away—probably Seenu, who specialized in orchids.

'I always knew you looked down at the rest of us!' said Kamaraj in a low, bitter voice. He bit off a piece of Thimma's dosai and chewed on it angrily. Kempu patted him. He wouldn't meet Gangamma's eye.

Gangamma said firmly, 'I'm not saying none of you is good. I'm saying Ondu is even better.'

'A god match!' said Meena. 'Let's have a god match. I demand it.'

'Nonsense!' said Gangamma. 'It's a waste of our time.'

Meena walked up to them, knocked over the bucket of blue lotuses and stomped on them. Hard. There was a sad crunch as the lotuses were squished into the road, their delicate fragrance turning bitter and dead. Everyone gasped. Gangamma almost wept.

'Crushing a whole bucket of innocent blue lotuses on a petty quarrel? Fine gardener *you* are!' hissed Ondu. 'We accept your pathetic challenge!'

She stormed out of the bazaar. Gangamma stopped only to give her other flowers to Thimma. 'I'm sorry,' she said.

'I know,' said Thimma, sniffing his flowers appreciatively.

'Pah!' said Meena, as Gangamma walked away, and stomped off home too.

The other gardeners bustled around excitedly.

'We'd better go ask the temple priests about the god match,' said Sachi practically. 'I don't even know when the last one was held!'

'Me neither,' said Kempu, 'but I remember my grandmother telling me that she heard that it happened in the temple courtyard.'

'The priests will know,' agreed a large-moustached gardener named Shankar who specialized in deeply-scented pink roses. 'A god match! In my lifetime! My grand-uncle heard from *his* father that . . .'

Across the bazaar the whispers flew swift and sharp, filling the air so thickly that even the pilgrims could feel the excitement—

God match! I've heard they have to shoot an arrow into a tree and bring out its beating heart . . . No ya, there's some special fruit they have to fetch from the South Pole! Ujhu! Who's in the match? That Gangamma, you know? Always been a little strange . . . And her new apprentice . . . From some outlandish place . . . North, I heard . . . North it seems! She's from the end of the world! But to agree to a match!

Of course, Meena has always been a little—sorry for the pun—meaner than the average person . . . What do you say we make a small bet on it? Strictly unofficial okay? Just enough money to make it interesting . . . So who do you think will win?

Part III

Chapter 1

'You felt *him*?' sneered Chitrasena.

'Yes,' sad Jayanti firmly. 'He is . . . was . . . he was my brother. Of course I did!'

'So he's alive?' asked Nala. He was a short tree-shaped yaksha, gentle and patient. Jayanti wished he would take charge of the sabha instead of leaving everything to Chitrasena.

'If you call that alive,' sneered Padmavati. She was mostly human-looking but her legs ended in a network of roots, and yellow lilies bloomed in her hair. She was almost as bad about the Outside as Chitrasena but she was generally a bit quieter. 'I think it must be truly horrific to live like that.'

'That was my worry also,' confessed Jayanti. 'That bird . . . how can it be Jayant? It could not speak, or change form. It had no magic . . .'

'But what if he's lived as a bird for more than a thousand years? That is not how ordinary birds are,' said Nala. 'Some magic is clearly alive in him.'

'Maybe he was only forced into this body recently,' said Jayanti, saying the worst thing she could think of. She wanted them to prove her wrong. She wanted to know for certain that Jayant was still alive, still himself.

'That chough is a petty thief more likely,' said Chitra horrifyingly. 'Probably stole Jayant's essence from wherever he died. It's an abomination.'

'Perhaps it doesn't know,' said Nala.

'That is still wrong,' said Chitra.

'If Jayant is trapped within that speechless, thoughtless bird, we must free him,' said Padmavati softly.

There was silence. They all knew what that meant. The others turned to Jayanti, their expressions half-pitying, half-taunting her to defend the bird. Her own Winged Guard eyed her suspiciously. Jayanti said, choking, 'We must free him.'

She took a deep breath. 'It's not just him,' she said. 'Someone there had magic. I think maybe one of the others was there too. They disappeared before I could be sure.'

'We must go in strength!' said Padmavati. 'Some powerful magic may be against us.'

'We will free him,' said Jayanti. 'We have to!'

Nala patted her back gently.

❦

At five the next morning, armed with dabbas of food, water pots and packs of cards, the gardeners of Giripuram started walking into the temple courtyard. They came in twos and threes and gazed around them curiously, and with a good deal of excitement.

The Giripuram temple was unlike other temples in that it had, to one side of the main shrine, a large walled courtyard into which pilgrims were not allowed. It was usually kept locked and only the priests knew where the key was. At the far end of the courtyard, a toolshed was built into the wall, topped by a large gopuram, carved with thousands of flowers and stretching into the sky. The shed was full of gardening tools. Spades, rakes, pots, stakes, watering cans, diggers, moss-sticks, clippers, hosepipes, grass scythes and a hundred other implements lay in heaps on the floor. The courtyard itself was paved with squares of smooth, grey granite. From the walls, the twelve gods looked down at the courtyard, each holding in one hand the Giripuram lotus. Other hands held—depending upon the god and how many hands it had—random animals, tools, plants, weapons and food. It was said that this courtyard was the oldest part of the building, perhaps the original sacred spot where the gardener gods descended from the skies and merged with the earth. Twelve temple priests stood around the courtyard, one under each god. They had small digging bars smeared across their foreheads in red mud, marking them as servants of the gardener gods. They dressed in sensible and muddy clothes, sleeves rolled up, pockets bulging with seeds. Their dhotis and saris were hitched up to the knees and tied so they could work with ease. They stood absolutely straight and solemn and silent, apparently unmoved by the way the gardeners were treating the whole thing like a picnic.

None of the gardeners could remember the last time there had been a real god match at the temple,

so the grandparents who had heard stories from *their* grandparents were much in demand. By the time Gangamma and Ondu walked in, most of the gardeners (minus Karthik and Renu, the other blue-lotus growers, who didn't believe in early rising) were standing in small groups, talking and laughing, and swapping snacks. Gangamma wondered if she was imagining that the place went cold and silent as soon as she entered. Kempu gave her a half-wave, so she went up to him. Meena was already there and ready for a fight.

'This is not fair!' said Meena, as soon as she saw Gangamma and Ondu. To Gangamma, she sounded exactly like her twelve-year-old self. 'There's two of you and here I am alone! I was always more delicate than you, Gangamma—you're built like a bullock! And your apprentice looks quite strong—violent, even.'

'I'll withdraw then,' offered Gangamma, much relieved.

'Of course you will!' sneered Meena. 'You always do this!'

Gangamma said only, 'Ondu's the one I said was better than you. If you insist, you and *she* can have a match.'

'But she's an apprentice! A one-week-old apprentice, if that. I refuse to compete with her. My honour won't take it.'

'Your honour is a brainless slug. If you hadn't wanted to compete with her in the first place, we wouldn't be here,' said Gangamma, losing her temper.

'You should accept the challenge,' Kempu said quietly, so Gangamma knew he was still angry with her. 'You were the one who offended Meena.' He wasn't entirely friendly but he was trying to help her.

'Nonsense!' said Gangamma. 'I don't believe in this. Honour indeed! Anyway, Ondu was the one who took up the match. And won't drop it, whatever I say.'

'That's only fair,' said a priest. She stood below the stone statue of a grave-faced tree god. Its face was long and grooved with vertical lines; hers was round and shiny but there was a resemblance there, lurking behind their faces, as if they were family somehow. She smiled understandingly at Gangammma. 'If you don't care about your honour, then you certainly don't need the gods to intervene on its behalf. You may simply reject the match.'

'I am rejecting it,' said Gangamma.

'We'll uphold it,' chorused the priests.

'Let's go home then,' said Gangamma impatiently.

'No!' said Meena.

'Your challenge has been answered,' said the round-faced priest. 'Pester us again and watch your garden wither.'

There were some nervous titters from the gathered gardeners. No one really believed in the gods but no one wanted to offend them either. They had all spent their entire lives honing gardening into a fine and precise craft. Yet each of them knew that it wasn't enough. Plants with the exact soil pH and moisture levels still died inexplicably while others popped back into life, furiously flowering even decades after they were dead. The gardeners weren't sure who controlled plants, but they all knew that *they* certainly didn't.

'We declare that the match between Gangamma and Meena is void,' chorused the priests.

'Wait!' came a voice and Kamaraj shoved his way to the front. 'I challenge you!'

'Me?' said the round-faced priest.

'Her!' said Kamaraj, pointing at Ondu. 'Dosai-hating snobby brat!'

A couple of the priests exchanged eye-rolls. Gangamma turned to Ondu. 'You don't have to do this. It's stupid,' she said.

Ondu looked thoughtfully at Kamaraj. It seemed to make him angrier.

'I challenge you before the gods and their earthly faces!' bellowed Kamaraj.

'I'm eight inches from you. You don't have to shout!' said Ondu. 'Fine. Let's start!'

'Very well,' said a new priest. She stood below a different god, a rooster with a man's face and a delicately carved comb on top of its head. 'Let's get on with it.'

The twelve priests stood below their gods. Each took from his or her pocket a pair of small dice. Then they each solemnly them before their god. 'Throw for the challenger,' called the rooster priest. Twenty-four dice rattled and fell. Each priest called a number, starting with the rooster one— five, one, twenty-seven, three, eighteen . . . it was strange, thought Gangamma, that all their dice seemed to have different numbers on them.

When the priests were done, they pointed to a square and said together: 'Challenger's square.'

Next they threw for the defender and soon Ondu was given a square too, a few rows down from Kamaraj but close enough to glare at him.

'Challenger and challenged are both rooted to their squares. You cannot move from them until someone can grow better roots. We declare the match open!' chorused the priests.

Ondu and Kamaraj stood on their squares and looked around helplessly.

'What roots? What should I do?' asked Ondu.

Gangamma shook her head. 'I don't know,' she said.

'But you're the oldest gardener here!' said Meena. 'The gods know you spent enough time sucking up to my mother, who would've known!'

Gangamma shrugged. 'Never told me. She probably didn't think anyone would ever need it. Who would've suspected that her own daughter would be sitting around challenging people to stupid matches instead of doing some solid digging?'

Sachi turned to the priests. 'Well? Do you know what they have to do?'

Though their faces were blank, Gangamma suspected they were enjoying themselves.

'Make it grow of course!' said the rooster priest, waving her arms irritably at the stone squares. 'You're gardeners, aren't you? Grow something!'

'Grow here? But it's all stone!' said Kamaraj. 'What if neither of us ever grows anything today?'

'Gardens are forever,' said a cheery-faced priest in a parrot-green dhoti. His god was weathered and discoloured so no one could tell what shape the stone had originally been. 'We have all the time on earth.'

'So we get, what, a year?' asked Kamaraj.

'If that's how long it'll take you to grow something,' said another priest, whose stone definitely had antlers carved on its head. 'Though we suspect that is pitifully slow.'

'Stop arguing and get growing,' snapped the rooster priest. Kamaraj subsided.

Ondu asked, 'What can we use? Can we go out and get seeds? Mud? Water?'

'Nothing,' said the tree priest. 'You are at the heart of the gardener gods' temple. If this is not sufficient growing power for you then you can both stay here till you die of starvation.'

'This is rubbish!' said Gangamma. 'I'm her guru and I withdraw my apprentice from this contest. Kempu, tell them.'

'So do I,' said Kempu. 'Kamaraj, let's go home.'

'You go, you will never grow anything again,' said a priest who hadn't spoken yet, a tall, dark lady who stood in the shadow of her massive crocodilian god.

'Any town you live in, the plants will all die. All you touch will be blighted.'

'As if,' said Gangamma scornfully. 'Ondu, let's go.'

'No,' said Ondu.

'You can't possibly be silly enough to believe them,' said Gangamma.

'I live with you,' said Ondu. 'If I withdraw, all the flowers in Giripuram will die. Your blue lotuses . . .'

There was a long pause as the gardeners of Giripuram tried to work out how they felt about it. Kamaraj lived in town too. Anyone withdrawing probably wasn't—but just might mean—the end of the Giripuram lotus. Gangamma knew what the right thing to say was and she said it even though she wasn't sure she felt that way. 'Better than you and Kamaraj dying of starvation here, trying to grow plants out of stone.'

'There's some merit in what you say, Gangamma Ajji,' said Kamaraj hopefully.

'If you want to withdraw, go ahead,' scoffed Ondu. 'I refuse to be the person who drove the blue lotus to extinction and blighted the town of the gardener gods. And my apple tree is here. If you think I'm letting it die, you're wrong!'

The gardeners made low murmurs of approval. 'Besh, besh!' they said to each other and to the courtyard in general. Kamaraj looked like he wouldn't have minded being the person who blighted Giripuram but was afraid to say so.

'Now that that's settled, please go ahead and grow something,' said the rooster priest. Everyone went quiet and watched.

The gardeners sat down and made themselves comfortable. Shankar had brought out a bag of peanuts and was passing it around to the other gardeners. Ondu and Kamaraj looked at each other, at their gurus, at the sky. Nothing happened. Ondu pulled off her blue boots and sat cross-legged on her stone, while Kamaraj stood stiffly, shifting his weight from one foot to another. After about half an hour, Kamaraj raised a hand.

'Yes?' said the rooster priest in a long-suffering way.

'Can we take loo breaks?'

The priests looked at each other.

'We don't know!' said the tree priest with a slight laugh.

'But you're the priests of the twelve gardener gods. If you don't know, no one does!' said Kempu accusingly.

'We're human too. This challenge hasn't happened in many lifetimes. The last time it happened was before Talakad was buried in sand, when the kings used to visit here! No one alive has seen one,' she replied.

Ondu made a choking sound, her eyes were wide. Gangamma looked at her with worry.

'In fact, we spent all of yesterday rummaging in our archives for old books,' said a friendly-looking priest who sat under a laughing heron of some kind.

'Then why don't you call off your curses? And we can all go home,' said Gangamma.

'We don't have the power to curse,' said the rooster priest. 'That is in the hands of the gods. We only know what happens to those who withdraw.'

There was a long silence.

'So these books . . .' said Kamaraj, 'do they specifically say that we can't take a loo break? Cos I really, really need to go.'

Everyone laughed, Ondu gurgling uproariously, her face towards the sky. Even Kamaraj giggled, though they could all tell how uncomfortable he was.

'Do your archives talk about people who died of burst bladders?' asked Gangamma. 'Or is he meant to water his stone in pee?'

The priests looked uncomfortable. 'Our archives are really vague, if you want to know the truth. They concentrate on the dangers and keep going on about how we're all bound once the challenge is accepted. They don't really say much else. We priests are stuck here too, you know,' said the heron priest.

'In fact, we'd also like to go pee sometime today!' added another priest. 'So you two better hurry!'

'Maybe we should pray,' suggested Meena. 'A miracle might happen.'

'You can give us tools, right?' interrupted Ondu, who had been frowning through the conversation, her mind clearly elsewhere.

'Yes,' said the rooster priest, who stood closest to her.

'Can I have a hammer and a chisel, please? Two or three of each. And maybe one of those long pole-like diggers, like you have on your foreheads.'

The priests brought Ondu a stack of tools. There was a pickaxe in it. She chose that and the most solid-looking chisel and hammer. She found the joint between her stone and the next, and began to attack it with her chisel and hammer, chipping off the edges.

The temple rang with the sounds: CLICK-CLANK-KALLLAAANG!

'Can I have some too?' asked Kamaraj as soon as he realized what she was doing. The priests gave him some tools too, and he also set to digging up the stone paving. CLINGA-CLINKA-KLAAA!

The entire hill seemed to vibrate with their blows.

Ondu had started first and soon she was able to use her pickaxe to lever out chunks of her stone slab, exposing the mud underneath. She herself stood on one half of the stone slab.

'That's not allowed!' said Meena angrily. 'They're defacing the temple.'

'The rules don't actually say they can't,' said the rooster priest, who seemed to be enjoying Ondu's methods.

'The way we see it,' said the antlered god's priest, 'is that if the gods really objected, they could strike her down with lightning or something. Since they haven't, we'll let it go. We're quite curious to see what happens next.'

What happened next was a large CREAKKK and Kamaraj managed to remove some stone and reveal a nice patch of mud too.

'Gharial,' said Gangamma really softly, 'do you think we could go somewhere and come back very fast with a plant? Fast enough that no one knows we left it on Ondu's square?'

'You really have no sense of honour, do you?' accused the gharial.

'No,' said Gangamma. 'All this honour is wasting my morning. I want to go home and get to work.'

The gharial chuckled, 'But I can't. If I leave from here, I can't come back here. Or to Giripuram at all. Not after that day you ran mad and I had to bring you back home.'

'We'll just have to wait till Kamaraj's bladder bursts then,' said Gangamma regretfully. 'I don't *want* something terrible to happen to him but it seems to be the only way.'

There was a *Creeow* and the chough flew across the temple courtyard. 'Here, bird!' called Gangamma, standing up and waving.

The chough turned sharply and swooped low across Ondu's square and flew away. On the ground lay a tiny plant. It was something in the moss family, a bright and clear emerald colour that seemed to glow against the stone. Ondu held it up to show Gangamma.

'Cheating!' shouted Kamaraj.

'*Gods strike down upon this cheater,*
Thunder lightning hailstones beat her!' chanted Meena, who knew a lot of this kind of lore.

Everyone looked at the sky, but the gods said nothing.

'Plant it already!' said the rooster priest. 'If you let it die and make us all sit around waiting for another miracle, I will strike you with a pickaxe myself.'

Ondu grinned and dug a tiny hole with the tip of her little finger. She put the plant in delicately and covered up its roots. She sat by it and stroked it gently.

'Okay, let's go home,' said Gangamma.

'Not yet!' cried the priests, 'the match cannot be broken yet. We need a sign that it has taken root.'

'And what's that?' asked Sesha interestedly. 'It would be useful to know.'

'The gods will show us,' said the rooster priest grandly.

Gangamma sat down again, grumbling about her achy knees. 'Might as well be comfortable,' said Meena, sitting with her. 'We're all going to be struck down any moment for this desecration. Digging up a holy spot! I knew you'd be the death of us all, Gangamma. You and your daft assistant!'

Gangamma patted her back. She could tell when Meena was grumbling to keep up appearances and was actually just tired and worried.

It seemed to the gathered crowd that the sun rose extra slowly that day, spending unnecessary amounts of time following its arc instead of getting on with it already. Gangamma's joints got toasty and warm and she began to think that sitting there and watching the tiny plant was not such a bad thing after all. There was something soothing about being so idle.

Kamaraj and Ondu sat down on their stones too. Kamaraj buried his face in his knees. Ondu sat cross-legged and straight-backed, watching her plant intently. Someone whipped out a pack of cards, and soon the gardeners were playing a noisy game of 'Lie and Die'. Only the priests still stood erect and solid.

It was past ten when the sun was high enough to spread its light over the tall courtyard walls and on to the floor.

By then the game had grown quite noisy. 'I cut your eight of trees with my snake of leaves and then I will call in my compost pit where I buried that ace of spades and I think we can all agree that I win!' shouted Saritha, one of the younger gardeners, in excitement.

'Hush!' said the priests together. 'The plant has taken root. The defender has won.'

Everyone scrambled up and crowded around Ondu's patch, where a tiny white flower stuck out of her moss, like dew.

It was the most beautiful thing Gangamma had ever seen. She almost burst with pride.

'Looks like your honour's fine then!' she said to Ondu. Ondu beamed at her.

'Thank the gods!' said Kamaraj. 'Can I please go pee now?'

Chapter 2

'Are you sure you don't want to go, Chitra?' asked Nala. 'I won't go Outside,' said Chitrasena firmly. 'Not even for this.'

Jayanti was glad. More than seventy yakshas had volunteered for the trip. Jayanti had known a lot of the yakshas still held a grudge against Jayant and the others for leaving their huge palace and going Outside in defiance of the sabha's orders. She hadn't thought that so many of them would be her friends and colleagues.

'That bird is not Jayant,' she told herself, over and over, trying to forget how home-like it had felt to fly with him again. 'That's a stealer of Jayant's remains and must be ended.'

'Let's go,' she said aloud.

A great mass of flapping black wings rose together and as one shifted Outside.

The priests and the gardeners came up to Ondu one by one and patted her gingerly on the shoulder, murmuring polite-but-suspicious congratulations.

'Good, good!' said Kempu in a ghastly attempt at his usual cheerfulness.

'Nice job!' said Sachi and Sesha—but they didn't say it to Ondu, they said it to Gangamma.

'Nice, ma, nice!' said Saritha, pleased to have someone younger than her she could condescend to.

'I've had enough stupidity for one day,' said Gangamma to Ondu as soon as Saritha was gone. 'Let's go home. I'd like to do some honest digging.'

'Can we make a new plot in the overgrown space behind the roses?' asked Ondu. 'I want one for my own.'

'We can make two!' said Gangamma, relieved to think that she wouldn't have to speak about anything except plants for the rest of the day. 'Let's hurry home!'

This suited the other gardeners because what they really wanted to do was to gossip about Gangamma and Ondu. They wandered cosily back to the bazaar, discussing every little thing about the god match and the peculiar way in which Ondu had won. The general consensus was that Ondu certainly had some gardening talent but that everything about her was deeply strange. It wasn't just her willingness to break the temple, her giant blue boots, her refusal to make conversation, or even her dislike for masala dosai—it was all of these plus her ridiculous bird and the uncanny way in which it had helped her win. Questions buzzed around all afternoon. How did the bird know to fetch her a plant? Was she controlling it? Was she part-bird herself? Or was the bird some kind of mischief-making spirit or asura? It was certainly like no other bird they'd seen, with its bright yellow beak and red feet. And if this Ondu person could control birds, could she control people? What maya was she creating? Had she enchanted Kamaraj's bladder so he couldn't concentrate? Worse—was Gangamma enchanted into harbouring this powerful magician?

By evening, the gardeners had talked themselves into a state of panic. They were frightened and upset. Something had to be done, they kept muttering to each other.

As the bazaar closed for the night, Meena turned to Kamaraj, who was still worrying that his bladder was enchanted. 'Go home, sleep. We'll do something. I'll bring that Gangamma to her senses. But tomorrow. Daylight is the time to face enchanters.'

Meanwhile, Gangamma and Ondu sat by their tank and looked out at the garden, feeling pleasantly tired, very full and sleepy. They had dug violently and made two beautiful new flower beds— when Gangamma was grumpy she liked to take it out on the ground. Ondu had made them dosais for dinner and they were perfect—crunchy on the edges and soft in the middle, just how Gangamma liked it.

'You should cook more!' Gangamma said hopefully.

'This is the only food I can make. I loved it so much that my mother taught me,' said Ondu.

Gangamma gave her a look but didn't ask any questions. Why spoil the pleasant evening, she asked herself—it can wait.

Instead, she told Ondu stories from her own childhood—Meena and the goat who fled from her and climbed a tree, Meena and the tailor she was apprenticed to for exactly two hours, the raft they built together and how they sank it. Ondu giggled appreciatively.

'She sounds quite nice in your stories,' said Ondu. 'Not nice, exactly, she was quite mean to that tailor—but funny. Fun.'

'She can be,' said Gangamma. 'She just likes to get all worked up. And that really drives my goat up a tree, so to speak, heh heh.'

Ondu laughed uproariously and demanded a tree-climbing goat of her own.

'Nonsense,' said Gangamma. 'It'll eat up the lotuses!'

'Gangamma . . .' began Ondu, a bit hesitantly. 'About what Meena said yesterday . . . you've been very kind. So if you really want to know more about me—my parents, my real name . . .'

Gangamma had never seen her so nervous and she felt sorry for her. 'Nonsense! Unless your parents are really goats who are going to come and eat up my flowers, it doesn't make a difference to me,' she said dryly. 'Now get to bed! Shoo!'

Ondu laughed and shoo-ed and soon light snores rang through the house. Gangamma stayed awake a long time, wondering what had upset Ondu so much. And a little bit of her couldn't help but wonder if she herself was being very stupid trusting the child.

The next morning, Gangamma and Ondu woke up late. For Gangamma this meant she woke up at five instead of four, but she was annoyed with herself.

'Will you make breakfast while I go get the flowers?' she asked Ondu.

'No,' said Ondu. 'I cooked last night.'

'Fine. Go get the flowers then!' said Gangamma irritably. 'I'll cook.'

She roasted rava and chopped some onions and carrots, and got on with the business of making upma. When Ondu came back with the baskets and bucket, the upma was done. The kitchen was warm and filled with the sweetish burnt smell of fried onions. Gangamma divided the upma neatly into two and put each half in a plate.

Ondu picked up her plate and went to sit outside.

Gangamma felt unreasonably annoyed. She had no reason to but she felt somewhat shunned all the same. She didn't like to cook any more than Ondu did and she had nobly given up the thrill of flower-picking to make breakfast. And did she even get a *thank you*?

She ate her upma and drank her coffee and felt slightly less grumpy. So she went out to see what her ungrateful apprentice was up to. Ondu was sitting by the pond. A few upma crumbs were scattered on the ground around her. But a large lump of upma, half of Gangamma's hard early-morning work, half-floated dully in the water, looking pallid and shiny and pathetic.

Gangamma opened her mouth. No words came out. She tried again, working her jaw and twisting her mouth. Still no sound. She waved her hands in consternation and at last, the words came. They were thin, sad words and didn't really express how upset she was, but they were better than nothing: 'Aaark? Why?'

Ondu shrugged. 'Not hungry,' she said. 'And I hate this sticky, tasteless upma.'

'Oh!' said Gangamma.

'Sorry,' said Ondu. 'I do like the burnt, crunchy bits that stick to the sides of the pan.'

'Mmmph,' said Gangamma grumpily, though she liked those bits best too.

Ondu said, 'I *am* sorry. I should've told you earlier but I noticed this and idlis are the only foods you make. I didn't want to hurt your feelings.'

'So you like idlis?' managed Gangamma.

'Not really,' said Ondu. 'But I can't cook, and you seem to know how to make it . . .' She shrugged.

'Have you been throwing that in the lake as well?' asked Gangamma.

'Not always,' said Ondu. When she had time, she preferred to bury it in the compost pit.

'So you *have* thrown it in,' said Gangamma.

'Well . . .' said Ondu. 'A few times. So yes?'

Gangamma wanted to scream. She hated wasting things, especially food. But the words didn't come. Her voice stuck in her throat and her face was going a deep purply red from the effort to speak. 'No. Throw. Food.

Waste!' she managed in an oddly stiff, echoey tone. 'Bad!
Haw-ful! No!'

'Okay,' said Ondu.

'Not okay! Waste no! If you don't like my food, do the
cooking!' shouted Gangamma.

'I *said* okay!' said Ondu, her voice getting squeakier as
she got more upset. 'Why won't you *listen*? And isn't it time
we went to the market?'

Gangamma breathed in deeply and exhaled in a noisy
hfff. 'You stay at home and start planting your new plots.
I'm going.' She stomped off back to the house to collect her
stuff and then walked to the bazaar.

Most of the other gardeners were already in the bazaar
when Gangamma got there. They gave her wary looks—
half-smiles and half-glares, depending on how they felt
about her in the first place—and didn't try to chat.

Gangamma ignored the awkwardness and sat down
with her baskets. She arranged the lotuses in their bucket
so their faces all stuck outwards at customers and a mild
scent spread across the bazaar. Then she took out her
thread and opened her basket of flowers, only to find there
was no jasmine. Neither were there roses. Nor marigold.
Instead, Ondu had filled the basket with strange, nameless
wild flowers, of all colours and sizes, mixed up anyhow.
There were a hundred tiny blue-purple flowers Gangamma
recognized as having been picked from the long spikes of
snakeweed that took over any empty plot they could find.
There were bunches of pale pinky-white wild balsam which
were wilting already.

'Floppy, useless junk flowers! Doesn't she know they won't last ten minutes off their stalks?' muttered Gangamma, furious with both the plants and Ondu.

She rummaged in her other baskets to find more wilting wild flowers—some yellow bell-shaped flowers ('Stupid weeds!' spat Gangamma), fluffy pink touch-me-nots ('Yuck!'), bright orange berries ('Thoo!') and, at the bottom of the basket, a sheaf of feathery red grasses.

Gangamma was filled with shame. She, grower of the most exquisite flowers, trying to sell such trash? She stuffed them back into the baskets and covered it quickly, hoping no one would see.

She was too late.

'Whattis *this*?' asked a familiar voice. It was Meena and upon her face, stretching from ear to ear, was the most hideous and delighted grin. Gangamma hated happy Meena even more than she hated normal, bitter Meena.

'Mistake,' she muttered gruffly.

'A mistake!' exclaimed Meena loudly, her teeth gleaming with joy. People turned towards them curiously. 'No! By you, the most perfect gardener of all time? Or by your apprentice, most favoured by the gods? The nameless freak! The one you claim is better than all of us?'

'Both of us,' said Gangamma softly.

'Oho!' said Meena. 'Not so perfect, then?'

'Being better than you doesn't mean perfect,' said Gangamma. She said it quite softly but everyone heard.

Meena's grin grew stiffer and scarier.

'But the gods smiled upon her just yesterday. Are they wrong too? Only Gangamma can judge who is good and who is bad, is it?'

A hundred replies clouded Gangamma's tongue: 'I only said her compost was better than yours! Picking flowers is not the same as growing them. The gods only said she was better than that poor sap Kama. If they exist. If that whole contest wasn't the stupidest thing I've seen in my entire life. And yes, I am a better judge of gardening than you, you vain idiot. Why won't you ever let me be? GO AWAY!'

What she actually said was, 'Anyone can make a mistake. The gods don't come into it. I must go talk to Ondu now.'

Gangamma got up stiffly, holding her baskets of wilting wildflowers against her side. She bent to pick up the bucket of lotuses when someone pushed her and the ground slid away from under her feet. Everything went black.

When Gangamma opened her eyes, she found that it was only a few seconds later. She was sprawled on the ground in the middle of the road. Her bucket and baskets lay on their sides nearby. They, her, the pavement, the road—everything was wet and squelchy with crushed flowers.

'See!' she could hear Meena say. 'She's lost her mind! She's become so arrogant she thinks she can sell this junk and get away with it. Snakeweed from the empty fields! And here I spent ten years developing my famous yellow banana-scented roses! She's mocking the gods! She's giving us all a bad name! She must be enchanted!'

'I didn't . . . I'm not . . .' began Gangamma. But she couldn't finish her sentence. She couldn't explain and ask for sympathy from the crowd. She felt furious and hollow. 'Gharial? Take me to the top of one of the snow-covered mountains we could see from Hansa's house,' she whispered to the gharial. 'The coldest, tallest, furthest-away one. Now!'

'I thought you'd forgotten me!' chuckled the gharial and the air went thick and soft and white and whistled Gangamma far north. And for the second time in a week, the bazaar at Giripuram was Gangamma-less.

Chapter 3

'Cold!' whispered the gharial. 'Cold, cold, cold.' It clattered its diamond teeth together to indicate to Gangamma how cold it was.

Gangamma said nothing. She pulled her knees up to her chin and sat on top of the peak, crouched and still like an unhappy toad. Below them and around them stretched a thousand mountaintops, each chill and frosted. Above them the sky was a pure, clean blue. Even the clouds seemed crisp and cold—as if they were made of crystal, not vapour.

'Can we go somewhere warm now?' asked the gharial.

'No,' said Gangamma. 'I have to think.'

'Can't you think in a warm place? I recommend Java. I've heard they have that vile drink you like so much.'

'Shhh,' said Gangamma.

The crocodile shhh-ed. They sat quietly for an hour till the sun began to rise, a warm golden-y colour.

'Shall we go home now?' said Gangamma.

'How?' asked the gharial.

'However you usually do it,' said Gangamma. 'You know! Everything goes blurry and poof! We're in a new place.'

'I can't go back to Giripuram,' said the gharial.

'Why not?' asked Gangamma.

'We've been there already. I can't magic us to a place more than once. I've told you this before.'

'You know, I'm actually quite relieved,' said Gangamma. 'Never to go back!'

The gharial looked at her strangely but Gangamma couldn't see it.

'What's come over you?' it asked.

'What?' said Gangamma.

'You love Giripuram. You love your garden. You whined when I tried to take you on a holiday.'

'Giripuram isn't the same any more,' sulked Gangamma. 'Gardening isn't the same any more. At home Ondu is sullen and weird and interferes in everything and ruins my routine all the time. In the bazaar the other gardeners hate me. I like this mountain better. No flowers, no people.'

'What's the next town to Giripuram?' asked the gharial.

'The nearest town is four days away but there are a couple of villages only an hour away each,' said Gangamma. 'I think Aanehalli is the closest.'

'Do you want to go there?' asked the gharial.

'No!' said Gangamma. 'It's so boring. No bazaar. They only grow useful things.' *Like food*, a nasty voice whispered in her head. *Which you never do.*

'Fine,' said the gharial. 'We'll just sit here then.'

They sat a while longer. Gangamma was furious with Ondu, but she realized that she did feel responsible. She knew Ondu truly believed that wild flowers were the most beautiful flowers in the world. She knew Ondu thought more people should like them. And she knew Ondu was rock-stubborn. And yet she hadn't checked the basket on her way to the bazaar. And anyway—Gangamma stuck her chin out—Ondu was *her* apprentice, not Meena's. And the baskets were *her* baskets to fill with whatever she wanted and Meena could stick her beastly nose into someone else's flowers. Mostly, she was furious with Meena, she realized. Ondu was a weird coot but she didn't know better. And she was willing to learn. If only Meena hadn't started picking fights and shoving people around.

'That Meena!' she said aloud. 'She's always been like this. Even when we were kids. She'd turn every little argument into a giant public fight. She'd shout, she'd shove, she'd call in her mother, she'd call all the other kids and she'd make sure the neighbours were there. And I'd always run away. Every fight we had, Meena would make a giant spectacle and I would run away up the hill. Just flee—'

Gangamma froze. 'What does it look like when you take me somewhere? What do the other gardeners see? What will they think happened?'

'I dunno,' said the gharial. 'Hmmm. I've never thought about it. I'm always attached to the ear of the disappear-er. It's possible we fade away but it would be a fast fade, given how soon we reach the new place. More of a vanish than a fade. I'd guess that we simply ceased to be there.'

Gangamma imagined the gardeners of Giripuram standing around as she disappeared in the middle of the bazaar. What would Meena think . . .

'Ondu!' she said. 'We have to go back immediately.'

'We can't, I told you,' said the gharial.

'How close can we go?' asked Gangamma.

'We can go well outside the town, to the foot of the mountain. That should be far enough, I think. But you'll have to walk uphill all the way. And there'll be pilgrims everywhere.'

'Aha!' said Gangamma. 'I know where you can take us.'

Chapter 4

J̇ayanti flew at the head of a great troop of yakshas. As they got south and began to fly over more inhabited lands, people looked up at them and pointed.

'We don't know if any others survived,' she told the rest. 'It might not be just Jayant—all twelve of them could be living these awful half-lives. Let's stay quiet. Maybe they'll be with him.'

She called some clouds to her, dark, large, and heavy with moisture, to surround the troop. People still looked at them but they ran to find shelter.

No rain fell. The storm of yakshas flew on.

The gardeners of Giripuram were shocked.

'She just disappeared!' whispered Sachi. 'How?'

'Isn't it obvious? Magic!' snapped Meena.

Kempu laughed. 'Gangamma barely believes in the gods. Learning magic? Not her!'

'Maybe not. But her apprentice!' said Meena, too pleased with her magic idea to let it go. 'That's why her compost is better than all ours. That's how she won the match. She's bewitched my cousin!'

'Gangamma has been acting a little odd lately . . . but I can't really think she's been enchanted,' said Sesha.

'That girl has probably spirited Gangamma away so she can take over her house and garden,' said Meena.

'Nonsense!' said Kempu but he said it uncertainly. Ondu was weird. She hardly talked. No one there felt like they knew her.

'Only one way to find out,' said Meena and stomped off towards Gangamma's house. The other gardeners followed her.

'Wait,' said Sachi. 'If something has happened to Gangamma, then we need to get Karthik and Renu.'

The other gardeners looked at each other. Karthik and Renu were the two other growers of the Giripuram lotus, and no one liked them much. They were terribly proud of the fact that they could grow blue lotuses and scoffed at everyone else—including each other. They were both very young—only about thirty—and had become official blue-lotus growers only a couple of years ago when the decrepit old ladies they had both been apprenticed to had finally died. In the time-honoured way of the blue-lotus growers, the two women had handed over their gardens and houses to their apprentices and walked away. The story was that they had walked all the way to the Kaveri River in the middle of the monsoon. There, as custom decreed, they closed their eyes, turned their thoughts to the gods and walked into the river, never to be seen again. Tradition had it that the rich silts the river left on its banks were their bodies. Their apprentices were allowed to boast for at least three years if the crops were particularly fine. Needless to stay, Karthik and Renu were still boasting.

'It'll take too long. They're always late,' grumped Meena—Gangamma was only one of many gardeners she enjoyed holding a grudge against.

'No, if a grower of blue lotuses is dead, and if her apprentice did it, then only the other growers can decide who will get her plants. We have to do this properly,' said Sesha.

'I really don't think we should panic just yet,' said Kempu. 'Gangamma's the strongest-minded person I know. And there's nothing wrong with her. Those two idiots couldn't pick a replacement for her if they tried for the next fifty years.'

'We have to do this properly,' insisted Sachi, and Sesha nodded along.

Finally, at well past seven thirty, which was terribly late for the gardeners of Giripuram, Renu strolled in with her bucket of blue lotuses. She was a round-faced, long-plaited woman with an air of permanent annoyance. She rolled her eyes when Sachi told her the story. 'I suppose I should go sort out the situation,' she said, bored. 'Thank you for letting me know. Do we have to wait for that lazy Karthik?'

Kempu swallowed the first thing he was going to say, which is that they had waited for *her* for quite a long time. He was still moving his mouth around wondering what to say next when Karthik arrived.

Sachi, Meena and Sesha told him the story while Renu continued looking bored.

'A witch apprentice killed off her guru? This is serious business. We must take it in hand immediately,' said Karthik, who thought that if he was pompous enough, the older gardeners would start respecting him.

'At least someone is taking it seriously,' said Meena, shooting dirty looks at everyone else.

'Excuse me,' said a pilgrim, who had noticed nothing but the buckets of lovely blue lotuses. She touched one of Renu's lotuses and smiled at her. 'Can I—'

'No!' said Karthik in a loud masterful voice. 'Our duty calls us elsewhere. You'll have to make do with marigolds from one of the other gardeners today.' The gardeners turned away and returned to glaring at each other.

The pilgrim backed away sadly. 'Have some dosai,' said Thimma kindly, from one side. He had heard the commotion and wanted to watch the fun. 'You'll feel better. Forget the lotuses, go see the gods.' He turned to the fight.

'What exactly are you going to do?' asked Sesha.

'Renu and I will deal with this imposter,' said Karthik.

'But . . .' said Kempu.

'The affairs of the blue-lotus growers are, as you know, complex and ineffable,' began Karthik.

'Come, Karthik! We'll talk as we walk,' interrupted Renu.

Off they went, Karthik huffing along with his short hard stomp and Renu seeming to glide ahead without using any muscles at all.

'Those brats!' spat Meena.

Sesha and Sachi looked at each other. It didn't happen very often, but it was clear that Meena was right. 'Those children might know about blue lotuses but they may not know much about the law,' said Sesha.

'And Gangamma was our friend,' said Shankar. 'Sort of. We should make sure that she is properly avenged.'

And they left too. Kempu followed, not bothering to justify himself. Kamaraj took one look and ran after him, not wanting to be left out. 'I'll come and see how these situations work . . . useful experience . . .' he panted. Others got up and left, not bothering to make excuses. They didn't want to miss the excitement. And soon the fabled flowers of Giripuram lay unattended along the street for pilgrims to sniff and steal and squish as every single gardener in the village hurried purposefully to Gangamma's house.

'How fast they went from maybe-weird to vengeance! Those gardeners,' sighed Thimma to his neighbour, the forest-fruit lady, whose name was Banashakti, Bana to friends. She had joined him at the edge of the gardeners, and had been watching them argue with a sardonic grin on her face. Bana knew more about plants and weather and winds than anyone else, and there were few diseases she couldn't cure—but there was something a bit forbidding about her, and no one would have dreamt of accusing her of being an enchanter. She was just too scary. Bana grinned. 'Second day in a row! Imagine how much the pilgrims would complain if we decided to take holidays and fight over some rubbish every morning!' She patted her fruits affectionately, glossy purple jamuns and translucent green star fruit.

'They won't hurt that child, will they?' said Thimma.

'No, they're all too tame,' said Bana, but she said it thoughtfully.

'She's an arrogant brat . . .' agreed Thimma. 'And Gangamma is worse. A little shouting probably wouldn't hurt them. But a real witch-hunt?'

'Not in Giripuram surely!' said Bana. There was nothing in her voice to suggest that she might be a witch the people of Giripuram were carefully not hunting. 'But I have to wonder, how did Gangamma disappear? I didn't see it myself. Something horrible is going on.'

Thimma's eyes gleamed, equal parts worry and excitement. 'Someone outside the gardening community should be there. Someone impartial—'

'You're hardly impartial after the way that child scorned your dosais!' said Bana.

'She'll probably like your fruit. If I go for Gangamma, will you come along for the child?' said Thimma pleadingly. 'We'll get a couple of the booksellers to mind our stalls. Their business won't really pick up for another hour or two anyway. And we'll be back well before the eleven o' clock-snack crowd.'

'Okay,' said Bana, who was sorry to have missed the god match and needed only the slightest reason to go join the excitement. 'We'll make sure everyone is treated fairly.'

And they set off too.

Chapter 5

The nicest features about the black, winged form were the eyes. They could focus on things up to five kilometres away and make out even the tiniest detail of form and face. Jayanti could see the little green hill ahead of her now. She was half excited to see Jayant again, half dreading what she must do. Ahead of her, she saw a black bird circling idly, high above the tank. It saw her and paused, hovering on the spot for a minute. She beamed, before realizing that behind her was a giant troop of angry yakshas. She held up a claw and beckoned the chough to come to them. It considered for a moment, but something on the ground caught its attention. It swooped down.

Jayanti paused in mid-air. Behind her, the huge clouds had stopped and the yakshas gathered around her, all looking to see what had upset her so much.

'Was that . . .?' asked Guha, who had been Jayanti's second-in-command for centuries.

'Yes,' said Jayanti.

'That tree!' said Padmavati. 'That's Mahendra. I can feel it!' She looked hopefully at Jayanti.

'We were never close. Are you sure it's him?' asked Jayanti.

'Positive. It's him and yet not quite. Like an echo of him.' She was getting agitated now. 'What kind of monster is it? We must destroy it!'

The other yakshas took up the cry. 'Destroy! Destroy the monsters!'

They swept towards the hills, too frantic to wait for Jayanti to order them forward. Only Jayanti remained in her spot, hovering. She shook off her indecision and followed them, faster and faster. 'Not Jayant. Not Mahendra. Just monsters!' she told herself as the wind whistled past.

In Gangamma's garden, Ondu was feeling a naggy, pesky feeling that made the mud a little less red, the leaves a little less green and even the flowers a little droopy. The air seemed unpleasant. It was guilt, and Ondu hated it. She worked furiously, and divided her plot into neat little beds in less than an hour. Somehow, she couldn't manage to summon up the feeling of triumph that she thought she deserved. Instead, she felt restless.

Part of her wanted to wander off, up the misty green slopes of the nearby hills. There were sure to be exciting flowers, and the chough could float happily on some nice draughts . . . but she also wanted to go to the nasty, noisy, crowded bazaar and see how Gangamma was faring with her wild flowers. Ondu liked Gangamma. Her flowers were fantastic, her compost was amazing and her garden was as perfect as a human could make it. If only she was not so close-minded about which flowers she should spend her energy on! Ondu wanted Gangamma to admit that her wild flower idea was clever and wonderful and that Ondu herself was a gardening wizard. Ondu wondered if Gangamma had opened the basket yet and been charmed—for she couldn't imagine anyone not being charmed—by her careful selection of wild flowers. She imagined the pilgrims thronging to Gangamma's stall as word got out about the wild flowers:

'This is a real flower!' one would say, sniffing a pale-yellow wild jasmine (completely crushed by then, actually).

'What are gaudy roses compared to these delicate blooms!' another would say, tucking a bunch of pale-pink balsam in her hair. And all the other gardeners would be filled with delight at the true floral excellence they had been ignoring for so long, decided Ondu. She couldn't decide whether to go to the bazaar and bask in her triumph (could she manage to not look too smug?) or to go to the hills and simply have a nice morning. Then she remembered that Gangamma had specifically asked her to stay at home.

Being an apprentice is no fun sometimes. Ondu decided to compromise by mulching around her apple tree. She had been neglecting it, she feared, and it had had to learn to live in entirely new climate, poor thing. She decided to dig up the mud around it first, add a little cow dung and then put her straw over it. It would take a good long time. She took up Gangamma's favourite digger, a long, sturdy iron rod with a pointy, chiselled end and attacked the ground vigorously.

She was digging industriously when the gardeners showed up, their faces sweaty with shouting excitedly all the way there. For one thrilling moment Ondu thought they were excited about her wild flowers. It didn't last. Meena was right in front, her handsome face red and sweaty. 'Is that where you buried her?' she hollered.

'What?' asked Ondu. Dreams of wild flowers and admiring pilgrims melted away, leaving her a bit dazed.

The other gardeners arrived, and spread around them silently. Bana and Thimma stood at the back. The sky darkened and though this was normal enough in Giripuram, it felt to Ondu as if even the clouds were gathering avidly to watch her.

'My cousin! She's gone! You killed her! You're some kind of witch, don't lie!' yelled Meena, a gleam in her eye. She'd been wanting a proper yelling match for so long. She kept trying to get Gangamma to yell, but Gangamma only sneered softly, went away, and then forgot about her. Meena was hoping Ondu would be a better fighter.

Ondu was. 'If you mean Gangamma,' she said, 'then shouldn't I be asking you? The last time I saw her, she was heading to the bazaar. If I had to name her most vicious enemy, it would be you.'

She turned furiously on the other gardeners. 'What?' she shouted. 'Why are you all here?'

'Gangamma disappeared,' said Kempu. 'Vanished. There one moment, gone the next. It had to be magic.'

'What?' asked Ondu again, unable to think of any other words. This time she said it with surprise and much less violence.

'She was sitting in the bazaar, and then she wasn't anywhere,' said Kempu.

'Actually, she was lying in the bazaar,' said Sachi sharply. 'Her dear cousin pushed her over.'

'What!' exclaimed Ondu, appalled at Meena. And at herself for being the girl who knew only one word. Kamaraj caught her eye and giggled. Through her anger and the general air of unreality, Ondu suddenly wanted to giggle back. She swallowed the giggle and hardened her anger.

'You pushed Gangamma over?' she said to Meena. 'Was she hurt? What is wrong with you? Aren't you too old to behave like this?'

Meena didn't seem to think she was required to answer. 'You made her stop existing!'

'No!' said Ondu. 'I like Gangamma! Why would I?'

'Then why did you shame her before all the gardeners?' asked Meena nastily.

'What?' said Kamaraj, joining in. He hadn't realized how much drama he'd missed arriving ten minutes later than usual that morning.

'Oho,' said Meena. 'Didn't you hear? Our Best-Gardener-in-the-World is so sure that anything she does is perfect that she brought a bunch of ratty, dead weeds to the bazaar today!' She smirked at Ondu.

'What? Those were fresh hillside flowers. *I* put them in her basket,' said Ondu. 'They were *not* ratty. They were delicate and beautiful!'

'They were dead. And unworthy of a Giripuram gardener,' said Meena.

Ondu looked around. It was clear everyone agreed.

'Weeds,' said Sachi, shaking her head sadly at Ondu. 'It hurts all our reputations, ma. But Gangamma's most of all. And after all she's done, taking you in the way she has . . .'

Ondu felt terrible.

'Renu and I would like to conclude our business and get back to our gardens,' said Karthik importantly. 'You all will not understand, but our lotuses will pine if we stay away from them too long.'

Renu pushed past Kempu to get right to Ondu. 'You're the murdering apprentice?' she demanded, with a faint air of surprise.

'No!' said Ondu.

'Our duty is clear, Renu. We'll just have to take her to town to a judge,' declared Karthik, his voice ringing.

'She doesn't look smart enough to be a magician and a murderer,' said Renu lightly.

'I'm not either!' protested Ondu, hoping Renu at least would be willing to listen.

Renu ignored her and turned to Karthik. 'This not our problem, thank the gods! Let a judge deal with it!'

They grabbed one of Ondu's arms each and started to walk.

'Wait,' said Kempu. 'You said you'd settle this. I never heard anything about judges.'

They didn't stop. 'We *are* settling this. By finding a nice jail and a judge. Maybe an executioner,' said Renu indifferently.

'The due process of law will be followed, of course,' said Karthik.

'Maybe we can find a gardener in Aanehalli to replace Gangamma and this brat. I hope we don't have to go all the way to Dwarasamudram,' sighed Renu.

Ondu said nothing at all. She walked miserably between Renu and Karthik, wondering where Gangamma could be.

'You can't kill Ondu!' shouted Kempu.

'Even if she is a witch!' shouted Sachi.

'*Particularly* if she is a witch,' murmured Bana to Thimma, looking up.

Which is when the chough swooped down and twenty different things happened in the same instant.

The chough flapped across Karthik and Renu's faces, calling loudly, its sharp beak scissoring open and shut and its claws sticking out. They panicked and dropped Ondu's arms to spread their hands across their eyes. The chough attacked Karthik's ear in an irritated way, a sharp clip to act as a warning. Then it snipped Renu's. It took less than a second to do both and to land on Ondu's shoulder and caw while Karthik and Renu yelled, touched their ears, found blood on them, backed away from Ondu and continued screaming.

The sound shocked the other gardeners into action. Kamaraj gave Renu a slightly muddy hanky with which to wipe the blood off. Sachi and Sesha turned to each other and snapped together, 'Now what?' Bana and Thimma had cornered Meena and tried to calm her down.

Ondu stood there, stroking her chough and worrying about Gangamma.

Amid all the excitement, the normally weather-obsessed gardeners of Giripuram failed to notice that a dark mass of storm clouds was approaching. It flew towards them rapidly, and as it came closer, a person looking upwards would've seen that flying in and out of the blue-and-grey mass of clouds were large creatures, black and winged. The gardeners only noticed when the cloud of creatures descended sharply around the apple tree. Some landed, large leather wings swishing, and surrounded the tree. Others flew above, watching the scene.

The gardeners watched in varying degrees of surprise, fear and curiosity. What were these strange creatures?

'Yakshas!' Bana said to Thimma, her lips barely moving. 'But not like any I've seen before!'

Ondu recognized them immediately. She remembered the long-ago night when her entire world had changed, the night she had been trying to forget for centuries. She remembered the yakshas attacking the town with thunder and lightning and earthquakes. Ondu felt sick with dread. What did they want now, after all this time? She stood close behind Bana who seemed the most comforting person there. The yakshas appeared to think of the gardeners as part of the landscape. They concentrated on the tree. They slashed and cut at its leaves with canines and claws.

'No!' whispered Ondu.

Bana stretched an arm across Ondu to bar her from going forward. 'Shhh,' she said grimly. 'Don't draw attention to yourself.'

'No,' whispered Ondu again, 'no, no, no, no!' Her voice rose, and ended in a yell.

The yakshas turned to her and something happened. A whisper passed through the group.

With a scream, the chough flew off her shoulder and threw itself at the creatures, too fast for any humans to register what was happening. It didn't even last half a minute before it fell to the ground with a sickening sound, more squelch than thud. Kamaraj looked away—he wanted to throw up. He saw that Ondu's face was sticky with tears. One of the largest yakshas said something, and the others moved back. It held up a large sharp claw and swiped, cutting off the chough's head. Then it sliced off the tree's now flowerless branches. It flew straight up into the sky, holding them aloft. Ondu flopped down. Another yaksha said something and then they all leaned in together and began to yank at the tree trunk, their wings flapping. The mud sighed, and heaved, and the apple tree was pulled right out. The yakshas carried it high up with them, until they were all a speck in the sky.

'Phoo,' breathed Kempu in relief.

But it wasn't over. With high screams, the yakshas threw down the tree and the head and swooped down to watch it fall. As it hit the ground, just next to the chough's body, the gardeners (and Thimma and Bana) flinched. The yakshas plunged back to the ground and attacked it again. They clawed and bit and tore at its roots this time. The smaller ones who couldn't reach its roots gouged deep scratches along its trunk. Others stomped on the bits of flowers and twigs that lay strewn everywhere. Those who couldn't reach the tree stomped the chough instead. They went on for what seemed liked hours, but was only about three minutes.

Ondu was so numb that she didn't notice that Sachi was making gestures to the other gardeners. They sidled out one by one and came back with tools from Gangamma's shed—spades, shovels, her long iron digger. Karthik who had gone last had come back with the only thing left in the shed—a hosepipe. He made strangling gestures.

'Go!' cried Sachi and the gardeners ran towards the yakshas, yelling and waving their weapons. They didn't run very fast, partly because most of them were old and partly because they were not used to attacking.

It didn't matter. Before the gardeners were even halfway there, the yakshas flew up into the air.

The gardeners crowded sorrowfully around what remained of the tree and the chough. Ondu crept away from them.

She felt alone and empty, much like she had the morning after the landslide. Her oldest companions, the apple tree and the chough, were gone. And more than gone, they had been torn apart and crushed until she could

barely tell them apart from the mud. At least she hadn't had to watch her parents being killed in the landslide. She thought with a slight pang of guilt that she had only known her parents for twelve years. She had known the apple tree for one thousand, two hundred and ninety-nine years and the chough for a few months less. Ondu forced herself to calculate it—she had known the chough for one thousand, two hundred and ninety-eight years, and seven—no, six-and-a-half—months. She remembered how it had arrived one day, a little after she had planted the apple seed in the high northern mountains. It had sprouted and she had been inordinately proud of its four tiny leaves. She was sitting and watching them, when a glossy black bird had flown down and landed next to her with a glorious swish. It had an intelligent, humorous look. Its eyes were bright and sharp, and it seemed to find her terribly amusing. Ondu had loved it immediately.

Ondu couldn't think any more. She ran. She fled from Gangamma's garden and headed uphill, taking the steepest, bushiest path. She ran and ran and ran.

Chapter 6

Jayanti flew north. She felt empty. Hollow. Now that the thing that was almost Jayant was gone, she wanted to go home and sleep and sleep and sleep. She flew mechanically. A thought stirred. It itched and nagged.

'Padma,' she said finally. 'Did you notice a girl there?'

'The one who reeked of Mahendra?' asked Padmavati. 'I was wondering whether to cut her head off too, actually.'

'She might not die,' said Jayanti. 'I last saw her a thousand, two hundred and ninety-nine years ago. She hasn't grown since the night Jayant and the others came to her village.'

'What is she?' asked Padma. 'We must end her too. Shall I?'

A part of Jayanti wanted to say yes. How easy it would be to let Padma slay the monstrous, undying, tree-dependent girl. Padma didn't think of humans as people—she wouldn't even feel guilty later.

'No,' she said. 'Let me handle it.'

122

As Ondu ran, she felt worse and worse. It suddenly became apparent to her that she was somehow responsible for the death of the apple tree and the chough. She had always known that this area was unsafe. She had been asked to go far away. And yet, having come back with Gangamma, she hadn't been able to bring herself to leave. Instead, she had sat around enjoying herself, picking flowers and eating dosais! She had been so full of coming back home and so busy re-learning how to live with humans that she had completely forgotten her friends!

'Selfish, selfish, selfish!' muttered Ondu.

She should've at least hidden the apple tree, she thought. And the chough! Why hadn't she had Gangamma send it back to the mountains—to any mountains?

Ondu couldn't bear to think of the chough. She ran faster, choosing the stoniest, thorniest, steepest paths, pushing her legs to move, her lungs to breathe. She climbed all the way up the hill, stomping and panting. At the top of the hill, she sat on the ground, hard, and looked down on Giripuram. What was left of the chough and the tree were still there. So was her new garden. And Gangamma.

'I'll go home,' she said to the wind. 'I'll tell Gangamma everything. I'll apologize! I'll cook. I'll help with the bazaar. I'll even be nice to Meena and Kamaraj. I'll make small talk with them!'

The wind said nothing. 'If they want me back, that is,' Ondu said to it miserably. 'They might not.'

'I thought I recognized you earlier,' said a whisper, and for a moment it seemed to Ondu that the wind was replying. The voice rustled in her ear. 'You shouldn't be alive!'

'That's true,' said Ondu. She turned and there stood one of the black, winged yakshas. It looked familiar, somehow. As she watched, it changed subtly. It was still winged and still about nine feet tall. It was now shaped like a woman, and its leathery black skin was now somehow *draped* over its body, in layers of intricate folds and pleats. Trying to follow them made Ondu dizzy, for they swooped and tucked in and out of each other in ways that seemed impossible to her.

'It'll never make sense, you know,' said the creature, amused. 'I'm a yaksha. Our eyes and minds don't work like yours.'

'That's true. We don't like murder as much as you do,' said Ondu.

'Of course, you're part-yaksha now,' she replied, and her whispery voice was now harsh and dry instead of light and breezy. 'Something of our people runs through you. You're polluted. I do not understand you. How did you become like this?'

'No!' said Ondu stoutly. It didn't really answer the yaksha's questions, but it summed up her feelings.

'I don't know how you did it. Or why,' said the yaksha.

She put out a wing and touched Ondu's pulse. Though it looked so shiny, almost wet, the wing was dry and cool, and long claws grew out of the end. Its touch was gentle. Ondu knew she should move away, but she simply couldn't imagine how this exact, almost-comforting wing had been tearing apart the tree and the chough just a little while ago. She felt too emptied to react. The yaksha closed her eyes and held Ondu's pulse in her claw for a couple of counts.

'Oho,' she said softly. 'I see. This is verrry interesting.'

'What? What is it? What am I?' asked Ondu. Her mind ran over stories she had heard as a child, stories where asuras and yakshas and apsaras and gandharvas roamed the earth. She was clearly not an apsara or gandharva. 'If I'm not a full yaksha, does that make me an asura?'

'No. More like a parasite. A sort of human-shaped tapeworm. A very bad one.'

The yaksha waited a minute for Ondu to say something and then went on. 'Didn't you ever wonder why you lived so long? Why you never aged? More than a thousand years old and you haven't even hit puberty? You fed on those people . . . I suppose they were just an apple tree and a bird to you, and they gave you eternal life.'

'They were the only people I knew!' said Ondu. 'They were *family*.'

'Well, now that they're gone, you'll die soon enough,' the yaksha said coldly. Ondu wondered if she had offended her somehow. What had she said? The yaksha continued in the same icy voice: 'But first we need to clear some things up. Ancient matters. They've been festering for quite a while. And you're our prime witness-cum-criminal.'

Claws dug deep into Ondu's shoulders and velvety, black wings unfolded across her face, blocking everything. She found her mind closing and going dark.

Chapter 7

angamma and the gharial landed on the summit of the Giripuram hill. After the knife-sharp white edges of the northern mountains, this green mound was clearly only a hill, Gangamma thought. Climbing down it was still quite a lot of work and Gangamma was feeling tired and achy. She could see Giripuram laid out below her. The bazaar was a mass of colours winding up to the temple, whose grey rock made it look like it grew out of the hill. The tank lay against the hillside, gleaming like the sky.

'I wish you could just take me home. It's going to take us so long to walk there,' grumbled Gangamma.

'Walking is good for your knees,' said the gharial. 'Or so I've heard. Loosen them up a bit! Make them creak less.'

'My knees creak because I'm seventy-nine years old and I have been active all my life,' said Gangamma. 'They creak from overuse, not underuse. These rocks are going to be their death.'

'Complain, complain,' said the gharial in an annoying sing-song.

'What do you know, you have no joints!' said Gangamma, sitting down and slithering down a steepish, scree-covered slope.

'Isn't that a bit undignified?' said the gharial.

'I spend half my day collecting wet waste and cow dung and mixing it to make compost,' said Gangamma. 'And I still have pots of dignity. Getting muddy is perfectly respectable. We can't all be studded in diamonds and get carried around by other people.'

'O Gangamma, soul of poise,
Your bum is making a scraping noise!' sang the gharial.

Gangamma laughed. It was a good rhyme.

'O Gharial, shining with gold,
I'm sorry your brain is full of mould!' she chanted back.

They made their way down singing their verses together, giggling, when Gangamma stubbed a toe on a root, tripped violently and fell splat!

'Slug-faced, leech-nosed, dung-footed!' swore Gangamma. She pulled herself up and knelt crossly on the ground till she got her breath back.

'Bones broken?' asked the gharial sympathetically.

'No,' groaned Gangamma, rubbing her toe. 'Not yet.'

'Good, because we might need to run,' said the gharial, suddenly quiet. 'Look up!'

Dark clouds were gathering above Giripuram. They were coming much faster than clouds usually moved. They had—and Gangamma hesitated to use such a sharp word for woolly clouds—*purpose*. They merged and gathered in a vast dark fog over Giripuram, strange winged creatures flying in and out. From the hill, Gangamma had a perfect view as the creatures flew down over the tank. They swooped to the ground and surrounded something. Faint screeches reached her ears as the creatures flew up, flew down again and, then eventually, flew off. On her ear, the gharial went cold.

'I don't like this,' it said, so soberly that it sounded like a different person.

'I know,' said Gangamma, walking faster.

The path twisted away from the Giripuram side of the hill shortly after, which is why Gangamma didn't see that a tiny pink-and-blue figure had broken away from the tank, and was running up the hill at a frantic pace.

Down they went, filled with a sense of urgency. There were no more rhymes and insults. The gharial kept clicking its teeth and clearing its throat as if it wanted to speak.

'What?' said Gangamma. 'Say whatever you have to say.'

'Those are yakshas,' said the gharial. 'This is serious. I think the apple tree might be in danger. And perhaps Ondu and the chough as well, if they are recognized. Depends on how much they know. They meaning the Winged Guard.'

'And what do they guard?' asked Gangamma. 'What are you hiding? What is going on? Why does everyone in my house know except me?'

'Ondu!' said the gharial.

Gangamma looked down, and sure enough, there was Ondu running up the hill path, almost directly below them. She soon disappeared into a curve.

'Tell me!' said Gangamma.

'It's the lotuses. It began with the lotuses,' said the gharial, sighing.

'We created them, my companions and I, but they wouldn't grow, they wouldn't flower. We spent hundreds of years but they simply refused to flower. They didn't like our palace. It's a . . . to you it would be hell. It's a bleak place, but most of my tribe don't mind because we are supposed to be concentrating on our insides. But sometimes we would visit the outside world and see the running water and the animals and all the millions of plants—ferns and algae and trees and flowers and grasses . . . You don't know what it's like to see them for the very first time at the age of four hundred and seven, which is how old I was. I'd gone Out with eleven others and we came to the Himalayas. We were sprayed by waterfalls and whipped by winds. But it was when I first stepped into a forest, with its deep, lush greens and its sharp, spicy deodar smell, that I really wanted to live there for ever. My companions felt the same, but we had to return. I couldn't get the sights and smells out of my mind—none of us could. We started wondering if we could recreate it inside our palace . . .' the gharial trailed off, for Gangamma was no longer listening. Her eyes were fixed on the sky.

Flying straight up, veering steeply around jutting-out rocks, was a big winged creature. Its wings were spread wide, catching as much of the wind as they could. Trailing behind it, looking a little silly, were long, skinny hind legs. What wasn't funny at all was that they were clutching someone. A small blue-and-pink someone.

'Ondu!' screamed Gangamma. She screamed some more, 'Ondu! Ondu! Ondu!' The black figure went higher and higher and got tinier and tinier until it was gone.

Part IV

Chapter 1

She had called Jayant family! What sort of monster was she? Jayanti felt a deep sorrow that made even flying seem like too much work. All the way home she kept picturing herself stilling her wings, so she and the girl could drop straight down on to the world below. It would be so peaceful, she thought.

She clutched the girl grimly and flew on.

When Ondu woke up, she was in what was unmistakeably a jail cell. There were walls on three sides and bars on the fourth. She was lying on a narrow cot, clearly chosen for its uncomfortable-ness. In a corner were a bucket of water, a mug and a commode. A paper screen stood awkwardly between them and the bars.

'Yuck,' said Ondu.

'You are awake,' said a voice. 'I have been waiting to talk to you for, oh, a thousand years at least!' It was her winged kidnapper. She shifted and changed into a woman, her wings and claws melting away; her black sari kept the high shine of her wings.

'It's you,' said Ondu. She said it without surprise. It was the official lady from long, long ago, and Ondu had spent one thousand, two hundred and ninety-nine years worrying that one day the lady would find her. She felt an odd relief to know that the worst had finally happened. She stood up before the yaksha.

'You can call me Jayanti,' said the lady.

'I call you a murderer. And I'm not telling you my name,' said Ondu.

'I heard the other gardeners scream it—Ondu! Ondu!' said Jayanti calmly.

She stood at the bars and looked down at Ondu. Her eyes were still bright and eager, so eager they made Ondu uncomfortable. She still looked both human and utterly alien. 'You don't look any older,' Ondu said finally.

'Neither do you,' said Jayanti. 'How is that, do you know?'

'I don't know,' said Ondu.

'I think I do,' said the lady. 'I recognized your . . .' she paused to sneer, '. . . *friends* you see. I knew them well!'

Ondu interrupted, 'You knew the apple tree and . . .' She sniffled horribly on the word chough, remembering how it had been killed.

'. . . and the chough? Oh yes. He was my brother.'

'Your brother?'

'Jayant, yes.'

'I never knew his name. He didn't talk—' whispered Ondu.

'You didn't know him at all!' said Jayanti sharply. 'That bird was not him. It was the echo he left when he was gone, dressed up as a beast. It was to my shame and horror that it lived so long.'

'So you just killed him off because you didn't like him being a bird?' asked Ondu.

'It was a mercy,' said Jayanti coldly. 'He would not have wanted to live without his mind, his swift-shifting body, his silver tongue! He could have fled from us—he always flew faster than everyone. He didn't want to. You saw him come gladly to us!'

Ondu said nothing. She was too upset to speak.

'It was a corruption of him. A spoiling, decayed thing,' said Jayanti, and Ondu realized she was almost in tears. 'Him and his stupid friends. They sacrificed themselves for those mindless lotuses. They brought them to your village, and fed them their own bodies. Disgusting, blood-hungry lotuses. We thought Jayant and the others were truly dead. But centuries passed and still I could feel him in the air, on the winds. I began to wonder, to hope and to dread. I have travelled the world following every rumour of magic—of crocodiles and trees, of blackbirds and stags, of giant frogs and herons being where they shouldn't be, doing what they shouldn't be doing. You know the kind of thing I'm talking about.'

Ondu said nothing.

'What we did—what we are doing—it's justice. Jayant and his friends hid from it for a very long time. When we saw what they had become, we were angry and grieved. Too angry. What we did to him was right, but it was not just. Justice is yet to be done.'

'What?' whispered Ondu. But she knew.

'We have to deal with you, of course. That tree, its sap runs through you. Do you know *its* name?' asked Jayanti. 'How long have you lived with it? A thousand years?'

'A thousand, two hundred and ninety-nine years,' said Ondu.

'Well, then you know how hard it is to kill. Yakshas usually are.' Her face darkened. 'Not like the bird. His body was fragile—so fragile. We couldn't believe someone could be so easy to tear apart. We are far tougher! Like the tree. After all we did, he's still holding on to his life. We uprooted him and left him there, to finish dying as he will. He's probably hoping it'll be fast.'

'How could you?' said Ondu.

'Your horror is temporary,' said Jayanti. 'You only lived so long because the tree needed you. You'll wither and fade too, soon enough. Your leaves will dry up and fall—'

'Hair,' said Ondu. 'I have hair, not leaves.'

The yaksha shrugged. 'Call it what you want. All of this'—she waved her hands at Ondu's body—'will soon be over.' And then she left.

Ondu slumped down on the ground. Jayant! she muttered to herself, trying out the name. The chough hadn't looked like a Jayant. Of course the last time she had seen him, he hadn't looked like anything at all . . . Ondu's mind was filled with images of the chough being torn apart. She sniffled and forced her mind away from him. At least the apple tree was still alive. She hoped Gangamma would come back to Giripuram, that she would know how to patch up the apple tree, that she would somehow make everything better. Ondu wondered what the apple tree's name was. How much pain did he feel at the moment? How much longer would he live? Ondu felt unreal. They had all been together for so long, and now only she was left.

'Ahrm,' said a voice above her.

It was another yaksha. This one was distinctly not human. He—at least Ondu thought it was a he—had the deep red eyes of a pigeon, and his neck was feathered in a bright blue-grey that gleamed green and red and purple where the light caught it.

'Your showing is tomorrow,' he said.

'For what?' asked Ondu.

'For being an accomplice to stealing the lotuses and helping the real thieves hide. You must display regret.'

Ondu shrugged. 'Why? I'm going to die soon anyway, as your friend told me.'

The pigeon man cocked his head to the left and considered her. 'That is true. Your human years are not very long. Yet you are no longer quite human. You have been *twisted* into something new and abominable. Our sabha needs to see you. We have been angry for so long. We need to know what really happened that day and who was to blame. And we need a criminal—any criminal. Two have been dealt with, but there were twelve. If you will shield them, then we will have to consider you. We think you have been polluted. We cannot take any chances.' He said it very gently, almost sadly. There was no sympathy there though. Ondu was already dead in his mind.

Jayanti watched Chitra walk away from Ondu's cell, feeling torn and depressed. The exhilaration of flying, of tearing and destroying, of not-thinking had worn off. All she was left with was the knowledge that the last traces of Jayant were gone from the world. Jayanti felt a deep sorrow, though she had done her duty exactly. Was this how Chitra felt, she wondered, was this why he was so unpleasant?

Should she go in and talk to the human? No, let her rest. Talking to Chitra was always exhausting. Jayanti decided to wait a little longer before going in. She stood straight and tall and stiff in her fearsome winged form, and she felt utterly alone. Jayanti wondered about the bird's life. He had seemed fond of the human, sitting on her shoulder when he could've been flying far and high. Would he have continued to live with her, if they hadn't executed him? Or would he have come Inside, given up the air to come home with Jayanti? And what kind of human left her world to live with a bird and a tree?

Jayanti decided she had waited long enough. She had to get to know this child better!

Chapter 2

Gangamma arrived home dirty and out of breath, to be greeted by a crowd of anxious gardeners, Thimma, and Bana. They poured out the horrible story of the yakshas' attack. Gangamma made sad and shocked noises every time someone paused. When they finished, they looked at her expectantly. Gangamma said nothing.

'And where have you been? Care to explain?' demanded Meena.

Gangamma said nothing.

'How did you disappear from the bazaar?' asked Kempu.

Gangamma shook her head. 'Not now,' she said. 'I'll tell you later.'

'Come, Gangamma. We will send these yokels away and you can explain yourself to Renu and me,' said Karthik fussily.

Renu merely smiled. It was not a very nice smile.

'No,' said Gangamma.

It was an hour and many unanswered questions later when the other gardeners left, muttering words like 'stubborn' and 'arrogant'. Gangamma didn't care. Only Thimma and Bana remained. Thimma gave her some cold dosais to eat. Bana patted her back and said, 'Are you all right, really?'

'I'm fine!' lied Gangamma.

'We'll come back and see you in the evening then,' said Bana cheerfully. 'Let's go, Thimma!'

Gangamma walked stiffly to see the damage to her garden. The corpse of the apple tree lay across the garden. Its flowers—which it had hung on to through its traumatic journey from the hills, into the tank and then to Gangamma's garden—had all fallen and lay scattered everywhere like snow. Gangamma sat *splat* among them, feeling numb and shocked. Her legs refused to get up, and so she just stayed there, worrying about Ondu, the tree and her ruined garden.

All day, she kept trying to persuade herself to go to the bazaar, to go into the house, to talk to someone who could help her find Ondu. But she couldn't. Everything ached. Her body and mind were on strike. She moped around the garden, not digging or weeding or even enjoying the flowers. She just drifted past plants, and sometimes she sank heavily on the ground next to them and stared blankly and unhappily inwards. She managed to talk lightly with Bana and Thimma when they visited her in the evening with food.

'People are saying Ondu was a yaksha, and that you were enchanted by her,' said Bana.

Gangamma produced a horrible fake laugh, a braying hyena-like sound. Then she swallowed some of Thimma's dinner upma—how she hated it—to show him and Bana she was fine. She chewed it violently. But when they left, she found she had no energy left with which to eat the rest. She continued to sit in her garden and worry.

It was past midnight when she sniffed and rubbed her dry eyes and stood up. She forced herself to eat a little of the now-cold upma and then, remembering Ondu, went out and threw the rest into the tank. It sank with a horrible, oily *glop*.

'What do I do now?' asked Gangamma aloud.

'She speaks!' said the gharial in her ear. 'I can finish my story—'

'I don't care about your story. Or those spoilt lotuses. I'm angry. And I hate everything and everyone. I hate these nasty-minded people and this smug, rotten town!'

'We can just leave,' said the gharial moodily. 'No need to sit around waiting for murderous thugs to come back and finish us off too. If it isn't them, it'll be some superstitious gardeners come to whine about witchcraft and attack some other innocent.'

'You're right,' said Gangamma. 'Let's get out of here.'

'Where to?' asked the gharial.

'Somewhere as different from Giripuram as possible,' said Gangamma. 'No people. No lotuses either, selfish lumps of dung! How about a desert?'

'Suits me,' said the gharial moodily.

Neither of them enjoyed the blurring and the moving. It was late afternoon in the desert they landed in. The white sand shone with the heat and Gangamma's eyes hurt. Her head began to throb dully. It was just what she wanted.

She stomped up a dune and gazed around. The only plant for miles was an unfriendly-looking cactus, its fleshy green stem covered in a layer of tiny fuzzy prickles and studded here and there with huge six-inch thorns. No people, no creatures. (Actually, several creatures including a scorpion were watching her and waiting for her to leave, but Gangamma's eyes hadn't been so good at spotting small things after she'd turned sixty.)

The gharial wasn't speaking, so Gangamma wallowed in the quiet. She was even, in a hideous way, beginning to enjoy the fact that the throbbing of her head and the itchiness of her eyes, in addition to her now slightly swollen knees, meant that she was too busy bodily aching and hurting to think about Ondu, the chough and the apple tree.

The sun set, and darkness came rapidly. The air grew chilly, numbing Gangamma's toes and fingers and soon her nose as well. Gangamma felt a bit calmer, imagining the night as a vast quilt of darkness and silence falling between her and the world. The silence was broken by some hideous crocodilian swearing in her eardrum. It was all hisses and grunts, and a light buzzing, but the violence behind it was unmistakeable.

'What?' said Gangamma.

'Look right-ish,' said the gharial, breaking off swearing for just long enough to get the words out, before returning to spitting out violence.

Gangamma turned and saw a caravan. It was a beautiful thing, a long line of light—camels and carts and people, all dressed in gay reds and oranges and silver. Their bright voices chimed and rang before them, chattering and singing. Some of them played instruments—someone beat a light deep drum, another clinked bells, and several stringed instruments twanged over them. The caravan was warmth and music and gladness, and Gangamma found herself hating it for seeming so nice and happy.

'Let's get out of here!' she hissed to the gharial. 'They look like they'll try and feed us and make us talk. Or worse, sing!'

'Right-o!' said the gharial in a bright, hard voice. 'I've had quite enough!'

And then the most peculiar thing happened. The ground fell away from Gangamma's feet and began to spin, faster and faster. Cities and deserts, oceans and grasslands, forests and mountains, icebergs and islands—all kinds of places flew around them. Strange people in odd clothes whirled past, waving spears and flags and—for some reason—tiny spitting llamas.

The world wheeled faster and faster. Gangamma went green. She was going to vomit, she knew. She closed her eyes and clutched the gharial on her ear.

'Blugh, gharial . . .' she begged feebly.

But the gharial just spun them higher and higher, until a new ground came up under them. Gangamma landed on her knees with an *ow*. She was kneeling at the edge of a smallish crater. Unable to help herself, Gangamma bent over the crater and was noisily sick.

'Happy?' said the gharial nastily.

'No,' said Gangamma. But she actually felt much better. Her headache was gone, and she could start thinking about Ondu now.

The gharial in her ear sighed loudly, its breath blowing into her ear, 'Hammaaaaaaaaa!'

Gangamma sighed too. Then she got up and dusted her knees and straightened her sari pleats. She looked around. It was a vast, empty landscape—just her and the gharial and piles of dust and stone and sand. The ground looked new and strange—she had never seen soil this colour before. She ran her fingers through it. It was silky and dry. The air felt . . . odd. And the sky looked different.

A thought came to her. It was a ridiculous thought, but it felt true. She asked it aloud.

'Are we on the moon?'

The gharial chuckled smugly. 'Good guess, though you aren't exactly right. This is not *our* moon. We're on one of Jupiter's moons. Ganymede, I think it's called.'

Unable to decide between scoffing and questioning, Gangamma said both, 'Hah?' Then she grinned.

'This is a good place, gharial. No people will ever speak to us here!' said Gangamma.

'That's the plan,' said the gharial, and they both chuckled, pleased with themselves.

'Impressive, huh?' said the gharial. 'Of course, this is just temporary. I don't think there's any food here. We'll have to go back to earth sooner or later.'

'What is your name, gharial?' asked Gangamma suddenly, ashamed she hadn't asked yet. 'I should've asked you this days ago. I haven't been very nice to you, have I? I just thought of you as a . . . magical vimana.'

'You want to know my name? Guess!' said the gharial. 'See where we are!'

'Some moon,' said Gangamma. Astronomy was among the many things she neither knew nor cared about.

'Which moon?' asked the gharial, sounding very amused. 'Huh, huh? You *know* you know this!'

'Jupiter's. Brihaspati? Your name is Brihaspati!'

'Guru,' said the gharial. 'That's what they called me in the menagerie at Dwarasamudram.'

'So you're from Dwarasamudram?' asked Gangamma, who had no idea where that was.

'I'm from a palace under the North Pole. But I lived in Dwarasamudram for some years. They were very nice. Kept trying to feed me—they never seemed to notice that I don't eat. Even you caught on faster!'

'Just so you know, I am sorry,' said Gangamma. 'Really. I have not been very kind to you.'

'It's okay,' said Guru. 'I've seen a lot of ears in the last thousand years or so, and most of them belonged to people somewhat harsher than you. The man you got me from was far worse. His turban feather kept tickling my nose and making me sneeze. He used me to transport his friends and relatives all over the world, and he didn't even try to feed me because I'm, y'know, made of metal. I like people to offer! So what if I say no? I was never so offended! I started taking him and his family to food places, hoping they'd take the hint.'

'Did they?' asked Gangamma.

'No! I'd brought him to the Giripuram market hoping he would buy me adhirsam, you know. Instead he gave me away!'

Gangamma put her hand to her ear and patted Guru. 'If we ever go back, I'll buy you some nice glossy adhirsam so you can refuse to eat it,' she said.

Chapter 3

Jayanti had never felt further away from perfection. She had never been one of the properly Inside yakshas, of course, but she had always assumed that over the centuries, her fascination with Outside would wear off. She would then begin to concentrate on her own self, until she hardened and froze into a diamond, so pure and clear that all could see into her and find nothing but light. Instead, she spent half her time longing to be Outside flying, and the rest worrying about monstrous part-yaksha birds and trees and even a human. It seemed she was more like Jayant than she had ever thought.

Ondu sat moodily in her cell. She'd been doing it for a while, but she couldn't tell how long. Everything here was the same, all the time—the air was still, and there weren't even any smells to remind her of the world outside her own body. There were no sounds either—the yakshas didn't seem to shout or gossip. Not around her, anyway, she thought sourly.

Apart from Jayanti, the one she had named Pigeon Man visited her most often. Others came and gaped at her. They gaped even when she spoke to them, and scurried away, as if afraid that her conversation carried some kind of disease. Maybe they all thought of her as a human-shaped tapeworm, thought Ondu, a parasite dying to latch on to them and suck out their lives. Ondu's favourite yaksha so far was the one she had mentally named Treeish—for he wouldn't tell her his name. He was thin and branchy and of all the things Ondu had ever met, he was most like a tree. Of course, like most yakshas, he wasn't purely tree-like; his skin was covered in a very fine layer of feathers, and he didn't have the green sap-filled smell Ondu loved best about trees. In fact, like the other yakshas, he didn't smell at all. Treeish liked to peer at Ondu and then disappear as soon as she looked back at him. Ondu even tried to grin— he reminded her a bit of her apple tree—and she thought he seemed nicer than miserable Jayanti and intense Pigeon Man. But he never grinned back.

Jayanti kept visiting with a new question every time:

What happened to the stolen lotuses? Where were the other criminals? Why was Ondu shielding them?

The third time, Ondu said defiantly, 'You killed your own brother! Why should I tell you anything?'

Jayanti had said gently, 'That bird was no longer my brother. He wouldn't—he couldn't—have lived as a bird.

So tiny, so mindless, stuck in one form for ever and ever. . . how could I leave him like that?'

Ondu had turned away and gone back to bed, unable to reply.

When Jayanti came next, she was her usual self again, and had more questions: *How much like a tree was Ondu? Could they test her blood? And why had the apple tree shared its life with her?* (She refused to believe that Ondu hadn't known it was.) And so on and on. Ondu found her so wearing she started pretending to be asleep when Jayanti came in, but it was hard because Jayanti walked so silently.

The Pigeon Man seemed friendly in comparison—he didn't speak, but then he didn't keep demanding answers as Jayanti did, either. Instead, he stood silently outside her bars, stared at Ondu and gave her what she thought might be a smile, a somewhat weird-looking twist of his beak. Of course, it was probably a sneer.

Ondu was beginning to feel so alone she started forcing conversation on the Pigeon Man. 'Why do you all hate me and want me dead?' was the question she asked most often, and every time she asked, he just cocked his head to one side and stared at her.

On one remarkable occasion, the Pigeon Man cocked his head and spoke. His voice was a soft, liquid *coo*, with tiny gurgles that made him sound as if he were laughing. 'Actually, I think I might not hate you. I don't *want* you to die, though I think you should. I think that means I don't hate you.'

'A dosai day for me!' said Ondu sarcastically. 'Dosai and chutney, even!'

Pigeon Man looked at her and for the first time, the red of his eyes dimmed. He looked puzzled.

'I mean that dosais are amazing. After I ran away, I didn't eat them for centuries. And when Gangamma gave me some, I felt I was home again. And *then* Thimma gave me one imposter dosai . . . it was soft in the middle and crunchy around the edges and it smelt of home. And he put potatoes in it. How could I eat it?'

The creature looked at her some more.

'What?' said Ondu.

'Such strong feelings! I would like to look at one. Can you make me one of these dose-things?' It pronounced it to rhyme with nose, the 'd' hard and thick.

'Why would I do that?' asked Ondu. 'I know some people eventually begin to feel sorry for their jailers, but I don't. Not yet, anyway.'

Pigeon Man looked puzzled.

'What do you yakshas eat?' asked Ondu.

'Eat?' he said.

'Food?'

Pigeon Man looked horrified. 'What do you mean?'

'Put. Food. Into. Mouth! For. Energy?' said Ondu, barking each word out impatiently.

He looked blank. 'Like you? Of course not!'

'How do you grow then?' asked Ondu.

'I just am,' said the yaksha. 'I was born like this.'

'So do you make your own food like a tree?' asked Ondu. 'Or drink water?'

'No, no, no,' said the creature. 'I am whole as I am. I don't need to add to myself.'

'So you don't poop? Or pee? Real pigeons do, you know. All over the place!'

Pigeon Man looked at her in bafflement, as if he didn't know what question to ask first. 'No! Never!'

'Nothing comes out of your body?'

'You mean like tears? Definitely not,' said the yaksha. 'What a thing to say! I remember you leaking bits of your insides when we brought you here. It was . . . unseemly. No one had warned me about this.'

Pigeon Man went away, but Ondu thought she had made a start. Next time he came, she decided to ask him about food for her. She wasn't hungry, but she was beginning to think it might be breakfast time. Or dinner time. Or even lunch. But definitely time for food. A proper meal of some kind, with lots of vegetables, at least two different kinds of fried foods, and maybe even some fancy rice with lots of peanuts and fried cashews.

When Pigeon Man appeared next, he appeared silently and creepily, and he didn't give Ondu the time to demand food. He opened her door in a brisk way and said, without even his usual beak-twist, 'Follow me, please.'

They walked down the corridors of Ondu's prison. They were long, narrow tubes, a dull grey-brown, smooth and texture-less. Ondu had to concentrate to stay upright on the rounded surface; her feet skidded and slid around with every step. She touched the walls, so slick, so smooth, that there was nothing for her to hold on to. She tried tapping, poking, scratching, but the oily, smooth surface seemed to slide away beneath her fingers. She stopped, and sniffed at the wall. Nothing. Pigeon Man's eyes watched her, head cocked to one side.

'You don't like our palace?' he said.

'I can't touch it properly!' said Ondu, 'I can't even smell it. I like things I can feel. I like them so I can scratch them and dig them and wrinkle them. This is frustrating.'

'I don't smell—none of us do,' said Pigeon Man. He laughed, a gentle guttural series of *coo*s, spilling over each other like running water. His red eyes gleamed, and Ondu had the odd sensation that if she touched them, they would feel like nothing, like the walls of the yaksha palace. For the first time she felt a bit scared.

She stared solidly at Pigeon Man and said, 'Yuck! I miss mud.'

'Oh, you are of the twelve!' he said. 'It could be one of them speaking.'

They walked some more. It might have been minutes or hours or days. Ondu couldn't tell, and her body seemed to have stopped completely, needing neither food nor rest. She didn't even want to pee—though her mind was certain it was long overdue.

Only once did they meet someone, a beautifully patterned leopard-like yaksha.

'Is this . . .?' it asked Pigeon Man.

'Yes. I'm taking her to the sabha. I'll meet you there. Hurry!' said Pigeon Man.

'I'll be there, don't worry!' said the leopard yaksha, its tail waving from side to side. It turned away from them and, as it turned, its body grew large and black and sprouted wings.

'We take that form when we leave our palace and go Outside,' explained Pigeon Man kindly.

'It was only . . . he looked so much like Jayanti!' said Ondu in wonder.

'She told you her name?' said Pigeon Man, looking at her oddly.

'She didn't seem very happy about it,' said Ondu. She still thought Jayanti was a murderer, even if not deliberately, but she didn't want to get her into trouble.

'It doesn't matter,' said Pigeon Man. 'Come, it's not much further.'

Eventually, the corridor widened into a vast room. Pigeon Man guided Ondu to the middle of it, while thousands of yakshas thronged around, watching and smelling her intently. It was not like any crowd Ondu had seen before. Bits of plants, insects, birds, amphibians, reptiles, mammals were all jumbled together and attached to each other, to form a dazzling variety of creatures, each wholly new and strange. Glossy feathers, scales and leaves gleamed among rough bark and fur. Voices chittered and whispered, clicked and screeched and purred. The sabha should have looked beautiful. But it wasn't. There was no mud, no water, neither sun nor sky. No smells. Ondu backed to the nearest wall and sat down. She felt something hard and chill against her back. She turned to see that she was sitting next to a statue. It was a small drongo-shaped yaksha, made entirely of diamond, blue-white and shiny. She put out a hand to touch it.

'Even you can't sully him,' said Pigeon Man. 'He attained perfection long ago. He is on another plane now.'

'He was alive?' asked Ondu. 'How did he . . .?'

Pigeon Man shrugged. 'That is not for you to know,' he said.

Ondu felt sick to think that she would probably die slumped against an icy diamond yaksha corpse on the cold dead floor, cut off from the rest of the world.

'What do I say?' she asked Pigeon Man. 'Do they know my language?'

'You know theirs,' he said.

'No, I don't!' said Ondu.

'But we've been speaking it all along. The tree in you knows it. If you hadn't spoken to me, I would have said you were innocent, uncontaminated. I might have considered letting you go back Outside.'

'Since I can speak,' said Ondu, 'tell me . . . what can I say to these people to make them less angry? How can I explain to them that what the twelve did was nothing much?'

'Nothing,' he said. 'Stand here. Share the ground. Let them see you and smell you and feel you and taste you.'

'And then?' asked Ondu.

'They will find the apple tree in you and then they'll decide that you must cease to exist. Then you will be dissolved. Unmade. Dissipated in some way. I don't suppose it'll hurt, since there won't be a you long enough to feel anything,' Pigeon Man said kindly. 'Don't worry! Soon there'll be nothing left of you!'

Chapter 4

It was morning in Giripuram, cool and fragrant. Flowers bloomed, idlis steamed gently, and the shopkeepers stretched and yawned in preparation for a long day of bargaining, selling, and gossiping.

Gangamma was not among them. She was still sitting in a sort of timeless misery on Ganymede, while Guru the gharial napped on her ear. She had got up once to pee into a crater, but that was all. No more moving for Gangamma. Her stomach made unhappy squelchy sounds but she ignored it.

When Guru woke up, he was less easy to ignore. 'I've heard you can survive about three days without water, and seven or so without food. We're running out of time. Are you really going to spend what's left of it on this drab moon?' he asked.

'I don't know,' said Gangamma.

'Let's go somewhere else, please?' asked Guru. 'We can even go back to your dull little town and spend the day digging. Your jasmine and roses will probably have started to wilt by now.'

Guru had said the one thing that could truly frighten Gangamma. 'That would be an unbearable shame. Giripuram lotuses, fine, everyone knows that lotuses are needy brats and will just die off on a whim. But killing roses is just . . . *amateur*. Incompetent! Only a complete slughead would kill off well-established roses in Giripuram weather and Giripuram soil, under the very noses of the twelve gardener gods. I'm not that dreadful yet! Take me back!'

'*Fiiiine*. Fine, fine, fine,' said the gharial. 'There's only one slight problem. Allow me to refresh your memory, O Gangamma, most gruelling of gardeners! I can go to a place only once. You know this. If you tell me the nearest village to Giripuram, we can go there instead.'

'Aanehalli,' said Gangamma. Now that she had decided to go home, she was impatient to get there. 'And you *know* this because we've talked about it before.'

'Where is it then?' asked Guru testily.

'Top of the next hill,' said Gangamma. 'There's a nice ridge connecting it to our hill. We'll walk down. It's technically not part of Giripuram.'

There was a moment of weightlessness and the air blurred and became blue and flower-scented and moist with dew. Gangamma walked down in a relaxed way, enjoying the breeze and the prospect of breakfast. Soon she found herself outside Giripuram. The sky was pale blue with pinky-orange streaks. The bazaar smelt of fresh jasmine, sampige and Thimma's first hot dosais of the day.

Gangamma breathed it all in. Then she ran home to see her garden.

'Hello plants!' said Gangamma. She could see weeds beginning to grow across her rose beds—wild grass and blue spikes of snakeweed were already sticking out everywhere. Touch-me-nots were crawling under the jasmine, sticking out their fluffy pink flowers. 'How long were we gone?' asked Gangamma.

'Who knows?' said Guru. 'I refuse to try and calculate Jupiter time!'

Gangamma laughed and went to hug all her plants one by one, ignoring the scratches from the rosebushes.

Then she knelt down and began to weed.

'I'm bored,' said the gharial after exactly one minute. 'What do you do for fun around here?'

'This,' said Gangamma. 'If I take you off and put you on the ground, you could help me.'

'Dull!' said the gharial. 'What else is there to do? And don't tell me to go to the temple!'

Gangamma thought. She still hadn't visited her lotuses. 'We could go to the tank. Would you like a swim?' she asked.

The gharial hummed in her ear. It seemed pleased.

'Let's go,' it said.

As she walked down to the tank, Gangamma could feel that something had gone very very wrong. Her throat felt narrow and dry. She swallowed and breathed in deeply. And she knew what had happened—the delicate smell of cinnamon and pine was gone. Her lotuses were dead.

Her precious, snooty, beautiful, pernickety, delicate blue lotuses had died.

A deep, black shock seemed to wrap itself around her. Gangamma was so sad, so miserable, so stunned and so very angry with herself that she couldn't say anything. She walked forward to the edge of the tank, down the twelve steps and up to the water's edge and knelt down. She stretched her hands out to the dead lotuses floating around in the water. They were black and limp. When Gangamma touched one, it came up and collapsed into her hand, roots and all.

'Oh, this is all my fault!' said Gangamma softly. 'They trusted me and I abandoned them. My poor, poor lotuses. I had one job in all the world and I ran away. I am the wickedest, most selfish person in all the worlds.'

Gangamma sat there for hours with her dead lotuses, wrapped up in her personal misery. She had failed everyone. 'I'm sorry,' she said in the same low voice to the lotuses, to Ondu, to the chough, to the apple tree, to the tank, to the twelve gardener gods, even to Meena, and to the earth itself. 'I'm sorry, I'm sorry, I'm sorry.'

The gharial made an impatient buzzing sound. 'How about breakfast?' it said. 'Nothing like food to cheer you up.'

'Food!' said Gangamma. 'I'm a murderer. I don't deserve food.'

The gharial thought for a moment. 'Not your own, certainly. No one deserves your food! My theory is that your awful upma is what killed the lotuses. Every time Ondu threw some in, one plant probably dropped dead.' It cackled at its own joke, but Gangamma was in no mood for humour.

'Probably true,' she said sadly.

'How about some travelling?' said Guru. 'Now that they're dead, you can't really do anything worse to your lotuses. You don't need to stay here any longer, pandering to their every whim. We can go for a long holiday somewhere. And you can eat some nice new food. Maybe even learn to cook! We'll steal new plants. It'll be fun!'

'No,' said Gangamma, though the holiday did sound tempting. She was still cradling her dead lotus plants in her hands. 'No holidays. Holidays are what killed my lotuses. I'm never leaving them again.'

'But you loved travelling! And your lotuses aren't really here any more,' said the gharial. 'They're dead. There's nothing here for you now. Except the roses and jasmine—because I'm sure the marigolds don't count—but you can grow those anywhere.'

Gangamma shook her head.

'Please don't ask me to go,' she whispered. Then she stumbled slowly to bed, her whole body aching.

It was almost afternoon when Gangamma woke up. She shook out her sari (which was crumpled and covered in a mixture of Ganymede and desert dust). Then she splashed her face in the water and said, 'Hmmm.'

'Food?' asked the gharial. 'Food smells are among my favourite things about humans. Even if I can't eat myself, not having a digestive system and all.'

'I am hungry, but I have one last thing to do,' said Gangamma. She went down to the water and cut off her dead lotus stems, making sure to leave the roots in, just in case they wanted to revive.

She waded out wearily. 'I can't throw them away!' she said. 'I just can't. Poor things.'

'We can cremate them,' suggested Guru.

'No,' said Gangamma.

'Bury them! I'll write a poem for their headstone. You can carve it in the purest black marble to signify your grief.'

'No,' said Gangamma again.

'Compost them?'

'N—' began Gangamma, for the third time, because though she wanted to say no, she simply couldn't say it. Composting was the one thing she truly believed in. It was almost her religion. The twelve gardener gods were just people to her, useful on occasion, but often tiresome. Composting wasn't like that. Compost never let her down, compost never killed plants, compost didn't play godly games with the weather and strike things with lightning (the gardeners tended to think of weather gods as random and chaotic, and ascribed all kinds of terrible motives to them), and compost didn't stop helping her plants because it was bored or on holiday. Gangamma still remembered the terrifying time she bought two bullocks for their manure and had to keep chasing them around while they tried to trample the jasmine, eat the rosebuds and swim amongst the lotuses. After four hours she had given them to the temple cowsheds as a gift, cunningly saying she'd clean out their shed and collect the dung every week. 'Let the gods handle them,' she had thought.

But that was a long time ago. And here was Gangamma standing in the middle of her garden, with her arms full of dead lotuses. 'All right,' she said. 'Let's compost them.'

Drearily she cut them into smaller bits and emptied them into the large pit at one end of her garden. Her earthworms wriggled with joy—for it was not often that they got such a rare and delicious food. Mostly it was just the remains of Gangamma's cooking, thorny rose stems and endless marigold petals.

Then Gangamma went in and made herself upma, which was the fastest hot food she could think of, and one of the only foods she could make anyway. She took her dinner outside and sat with her feet in the tank's cool— though sadly lotus-less water—and began to eat.

'Guru,' she said. 'Remember the story you were going to tell me when Ondu was kidnapped? Tell me now.'

'It's . . . I'm not sure whether to tell it,' said the gharial. 'When we were interrupted, I knew it was too late. There's nothing I can do now.'

'You know where Ondu is!' said Gangamma. 'You know who took her. You know why. *Tell* me! I've ruined a lot of things. The lotuses may or may not come back. That is their will. But Ondu needs help. I took responsibility for her. Kidnapped her even. We need to find her.'

'I know,' said the gharial. 'I just don't know what to do.'

'Tell me the story,' said Gangamma. 'I'll try not to interrupt.'

'I have wanted to. And not wanted to,' said Guru.

'Is it because you can't take me wherever Ondu's gone?'

'Not exactly.'

'So you *can* go there?'

'I can. But if we go there I will not return. And without me, I don't know how you will return—assuming they let you. Which they may not.'

'Who is they?'

'My people . . . the word you have for us is yakshas, though we are not as your stories say. Not all of us anyway. My tribe, especially, is very . . . *particular*. We like things to be clean, pure. We believe that we exist to separate our bodies from the world. When we are wholly separate, it is said, we harden into clear diamond and ascend to a higher plane. We live deep under the polar ice cap, in a palace made of a material we created millennia ago. It's strong and smooth and utterly neutral—your eyes slide off it as do your fingers. Even your feet make no sound on it. We believe that going Outside the palace will contaminate us. We think if we live too much in the world, we cannot ascend to the higher plane.'

'*What* higher plane?' muttered Gangamma rudely.

'I'm the wrong person to ask,' said Guru seriously. 'I was in no hurry to ascend. Yakshas who do succeed turn to clear, hard crystal and never move again. They don't talk or laugh or sing. I was centuries old the first time I went Out. I went with eleven others—we wanted to see what it was like. We knew that most other yakshas lived on the earth. We grew large black wings and wished ourselves into the sky and flew.

We were flying above the Himalayas when all twelve of us realized we simply had to land. I can't describe to you how it is to feel the wind for the very first time, to smell the pines and the flowers, to stand under a waterfall's spray. When we returned home, we took some flowers with us and tried to grow them, but nothing would live in our palace.

'So we bred the blue lotuses secretly. Of course, they didn't flower, because our palace has neither sun nor air nor mud—just dry sand. They needed nutrition, so we did something very foolish—we gave the lotuses our blood. Just small amounts. And they put out leaves! We wanted to plant them outside, but our sabha discovered that we were harming our bodies to feed the lotuses. They decided the lotuses were contaminated. They wanted to kill them all, rather than plant them in the ground and let them live. The twelve of us ran away with our plants and planted them here, in your tank.'

'Twelve!' said Gangamma, and her mind went back to the god match and the weathered stone shapes along the courtyard walls. 'And one of you is vaguely deer-like, perhaps? And another is not unlike a big black rooster?'

'I was wondering if you'd spot that. I didn't even know someone had decided we were gods. I almost screamed with laughter when we went in to the temple for the god match. When we planted the lotuses, we gave the tank our bodies to feed them. We thought that way the others would never find us or the lotuses. Ondu was there.'

'Ondu? She's ten! Maybe eleven? Twelve at the most.'

'She's one thousand, three hundred and eleven years old.'

'How?' exclaimed Gangamma.

'I'm coming to it. The tank took our bodies but it didn't absorb all of us. Somehow, either it or the lotuses or the blood-magic put us out in new forms. I don't know how or why—I don't even know if all twelve of us emerged, or only the three you've met. Ondu saw us going in, and she was there when the other yakshas came after us. We could feel them come closer, and I think they could tell we were around somewhere. We don't smell like you do, but we can sense other yakshas from our tribe. Usually the better we know another yaksha, the more strongly we sense their presence. This sense . . . it's more somewhere between feel and taste. It's as if our bodies know when a yaksha we are close to is around. So they knew we were here-ish, but they couldn't pinpoint us. They destroyed half the hillside searching for us. When they left, I tried to get Ondu to pick me up. She saw me—but she was suspicious. I think I sparkled too much for her. Then she found the apple seed that was all that was left of my companion. He looked like a tree, you see. She fled this place, carried it far north, and planted it there.'

'So you and Ondu recognized each other! And decided not to mention it. I knew there was something!' said Gangamma.

'Yes,' said the gharial. 'Back then, when she left, I was afraid I was doomed to stay underwater for ever. I was still in the tank when one of my friends hatched out of a coot's nest. He had become a large black alpine bird and flew north to be with Ondu and her tree. I lay waiting in the water for someone to pick me up and finally someone did. She wished to travel and I found I could take her anywhere. I've been wandering the world ever since. By the time I met you, I'd almost forgotten this part of my life. But your bazaar felt like home, and your garden smelt of pine and cinnamon. Slowly, I began to remember. In fact, I didn't recognize the apple tree when we first met, but you spotted that it was special immediately.'

'I'd be a fine gardener if I couldn't tell a tree from a yaksha,' said Gangamma stoutly.

'You knew?' The gharial sounded impressed.

'No,' she admitted. 'But there was something about that tree. I knew I had to bring it home.'

The gharial said nothing.

'Tell me something,' said Gangamma. 'How did your people find us?'

'I don't know. I think maybe the clouds spotted the tree or the chough flying through them. It's been so long since I was a yaksha, I'd forgotten that clouds could be spying on us.'

'And who would notice an extra cloud or two in Giripuram?' asked Gangamma.

'Yakshas would. We can speak to them and they oblige us. We can bring rain and thunder and lightning. They even act as our sentries at home. And the chough's sister—Jayanti—she was always sharp. She would not stand for her brother flying around as a weak, wordless bird—she would see him dead first!'

'Why? What's wrong with that?' asked Gangamma, puzzled.

'I told you,' said the gharial. 'Yakshas—my yakshas—we don't understand living creatures. We don't understand eating and growing and excreting. I do, but it was considered gross. Gross bordering on mad, bordering on dangerous. The others think it's icky and wrong to constantly let the world into your body and your body into the world. But with the lotuses, especially, they were very upset. Because we were feeding them with our bodies, our actual selves. The lotuses are powerful. They give happiness, yes, but it's a temporary thing, we all know that. And they feed on people. They feed on your spirit and their bodies, and they won't let you die.'

'Like the apple tree and Ondu?'

'Not entirely. That is more mutual. The lotuses . . . your guru, the gardener before you, what was she like?'

'Stubborn,' said Gangamma. 'She was my aunt, you know. She fought her husband and daughter to make me her apprentice instead of Meena. She didn't care how they felt or what they said. She didn't care how unhappy I was, as long as I did my work well. And she fought me every morning to do everything a certain way, at a certain time, in a certain order. She was self-willed. So sure of herself. Never listened to anything anyone else said. Arrogant, you could say.' Meena's voice echoed in her head, spitting out the same accusations about her, about Ondu, about Karthik and Renu. All stubborn, all self-willed.

The gharial's voice chimed in, 'As are all growers of blue lotuses. You need the will, for the lotuses take all your care, all your hope. And did you have some kind of initiation ceremony, something involving blood? A cut perhaps? Blood spilt into the water to introduce yourself to the lotuses?'

'We're not supposed to talk about it,' said Gangamma. 'But yes. There was something like that.'

'And how did your predecessor die?'

'She walked into the river until she drowned.'

'And where was that?'

'Upstream. A little outside town. Before the river enters the tank,' whispered Gangamma.

'And her guru too?'

'And hers before her. All the growers of the blue lotus die in the same way,' said Gangamma. 'In a few years I will too.'

The gharial sighed into her ear. 'That's why my people didn't want to plant them here. They thought us cutting ourselves was evil. We bred the lotuses in little jars, originally, but they never grew. Then one day I snuck out and brought back some mud. I called the others, and we took the lotuses out of their jars, packed the jars with mud and replanted the lotuses in the mud. My hands were bleeding, I must've cut them while travelling or digging. I didn't even notice, but the others smelt it in the mud. And so did the lotuses. Almost immediately, the lotus I was planting began to sprout tiny, spring-green leaves. That's when we all started giving them blood. They were bloodthirsty plants, but they were so lovely. We thought it was unfair to keep them out of the air, out of the mud and the water. So we brought them here and gave them our bodies, so they could live out their lives in the mud, with air and sun and rain.'

'I do not regret it either,' said Gangamma after a little while. 'Giving them blood, I mean. I've seen how they banish sorrow. One sniff, two, and the world is a better place. Even if it's only for a few minutes. And they *are* beautiful.'

'I suppose some stubborn, arrogant gardener with more self-worth than brains first gave them blood and learnt to live with the lotuses. And passed them on to another. They like Giripuram,' said the gharial. 'We never did succeed in making them flower. But you did. Humans, I mean. There are more of them than I imagined. And their scent is everywhere.'

They fell silent and then Gangamma said, 'Those flying creatures, the tree, the bird, you . . . what shape are yakshas really?'

'Lots of different shapes. And we can change—all yakshas do, moving through different forms depending on where they are. Among my tribe, though, it is not encouraged, because most of my people see it as opening up our bodies to impurities. We are allowed to take the black, winged form if we need to travel out of our home. But otherwise, we're encouraged to sit still and focus on our inner selves.'

'So what do you really look like?' asked Gangamma curious.

'Me? I used to be large. Really large. Twelve feet tall, maybe. A bit gharial-like but also a bit human. I don't know how to describe it,' said Guru.

'How did you . . . ?' asked Gangamma, waving her hands around, unable to ask how a giant yaksha had become a tiny jewelled gharial.

Guru laughed, seeming to understand. 'We aren't easy to kill. And we originally grew from the earth, much like the lotuses. The lotuses also helped, I think. After I drowned myself, I suddenly awoke in this body. Just as my tree-ish friend became a seed. And the friend who had liked to fly became an actual bird, an alpine chough. I wouldn't be surprised if all twelve us are still around somewhere.' It spoke as if it was perfectly logical.

It made no sense to Gangamma. She shook it off and asked instead, 'Could you take me to Ondu and then leave immediately? You will only be there an instant. I will figure out a way to come home. Maybe you can draw me a map.'

'Mmmm,' said the gharial. 'We have no doors in or out. Not as you know them. And the palace is far north and deep underground. You would freeze long before you found a way out.'

'I still feel like I should try,' said Gangamma.

'Hmm. Then we'd better hurry. I don't think they'll harm her but you never know. I never did understand my people. To get so upset over a bunch of plants! And we did too, us twelve. And now you and Ondu are all messed up because of it. *Plants!*'

'I will still feed them my body when I am ready to die,' said Gangamma. 'The lotuses, I mean. Maybe they'll revive then.'

The gharial laughed aloud. 'Of course you will!' it said, and suddenly it was the cheerful travelling earring who had hollered Gangamma into taking her very first holiday just ten days or so ago. 'I'll take you,' said the gharial. 'Let's go find Ondu. We'll storm that hideous palace, shall we?'

'Yes,' said Gangamma. 'But if I die—and I'm very old, I could die any moment—you have to try and bring my body back for the lotuses. Don't made a fuss! But if you can, then bring it back and put it in the tank.'

'Always looking on the bright side, no?' laughed the gharial.

'I mean it,' said Gangamma soberly.

'Then we'll make a pact. If you survive me, then you try—but not too hard—to put my remains in the tank. And if I survive and you die, I'll do the same. Deal?'

'Deal,' laughed Gangamma.

'Let's go rescue Ondu. And I think my friend the chough showed us how. When shall we go?'

'Now,' said Gangamma.

The gharial chuckled, 'I can't promise we'll reach now, though. Time is different there. So different, so slow—till we grew the lotuses, we didn't even realize that time was a thing, and could be measured and counted. I sometimes wonder whether the reason the lotuses didn't bloom Inside is that they simply didn't have enough time . . .?'

And the world sped past in a whirl of white.

Chapter 5

Jayanti watched Ondu come in. She looked terrified and out of place and very tiny among the large yakshas. Next to her, Chitrasena looked so smug that Jayanti felt a sudden surge of anger. He had looked exactly this way when he declared that Jayant and his friends had to die— and the same way when they had decided to kill Jayant a second time. She looked at Nala, who wore his usual vague and faraway look. Useless, Jayanti realized sadly— just like all the other people in the sabha. He was too busy concentrating upon his own self to act for someone else. He would just look kind and sad and let Chitra do whatever he wanted.

Ondu stood in the smooth and smell-less hall and gaped around at the gathered people. They stared serenely back at her.

Jayanti came up to her and said formally, 'Welcome to our sabha.'

'What was the tree's name?' demanded Ondu, relieved to have someone to be angry with.

'That is not relevant,' said Jayanti. 'You may address the sabha now.'

She moved back into the crown and watched Ondu, who was clearly angry.

Ondu looked at Pigeon Man.

'Go on!' he said encouragingly. 'You'll be better when you tell us what you did.'

'I didn't do anything to you!' she said.

'Part of you did,' said Pigeon Man. 'The tree and you are bound together. We hurt you, we hurt it.'

'It didn't do anything particularly awful either,' said Ondu. 'It stole some plants. I steal plants all the time. I steal seeds, I steal cuttings. I take fruit and flowers. It's called being a gardener. It's a job!'

To Ondu's astonishment, Jayanti held up her hand. 'That is a fair point,' she said. 'The twelve were doing their jobs.'

'Gardener is not a job we recognize,' said a colourful person, who seemed to be part-fish, part-plant.

'But *cultivator* is,' said Treeish.

'We cultivate the internal, not the external,' said another, a snowy-white egret-shaped person.

'The twelve were not cultivators. They were wasting their essence on trivialities,' said a third, a large elephantine creature that towered over the others.

'Hey!' said Ondu. 'I'm not a triviality. If I don't mind not dying, it's none of your business.'

'Not dying is unnatural to your kind,' said Pigeon Man. 'You have not grown in one thousand and three hundred years.'

'A thousand, two hundred and ninety-nine!' snapped Ondu.

Pigeon Man went on serenely, as if she hadn't spoken. 'You eat and excrete like your kind, but you don't get taller or fatter or older.'

Again, Jayanti interrupted, surprising Ondu. 'I think, in her case, we must show *mercy*. A thousand, three hundred and eleven years old, and she will never reproduce like the rest of her kind. She will have no descendants, no true immortality as they see it. Long life is a meagre consolation.'

Ondu suddenly felt hopeless. And like a complete freak.

'Are you arguing for growth?' Pigeon Man turned to Jayanti in horror.

'Not for us. For them. For her,' replied Jayanti. 'She eats, she excretes. Her body is frozen as a child's, though her mind is old. She can never die, but she will never ascend either. What does she have to live for?'

The whole room eyed Ondu with pity, all obviously wondering what she had to live for. Ondu felt both furious and on the verge of tears.

She was still wavering between them when there was a crash of smooth ceiling, and Gangamma stumbled onto the floor.

'Ondu!' she said, and gave her a large and toothy smile.

Ondu ran up to her, feeling suddenly happy. 'What are you doing here?' she asked.

'Rescuing you. Clearly,' said Gangamma, picking herself off the floor slowly. Everything hurt. 'Aaaargh,' she said, massaging a knee.

'Sorry, I'd forgotten the exact angle at which to enter,' said the gharial.

The crowd of yakshas seemed to hear him. They leaned forward, and stared eagerly at Gangamma.

'Is that . . .?'

'The gall!'

'Magma below!'

Everyone turned to Gangamma. She patted her gharial earring and said to the sabha at large, 'Guru here would like to talk to you.'

'Guru?' said Pigeon Man in horror. He walked up to Gangamma and peered at her ear. She shifted back a bit, uncomfortable to find his sharp beak so close to her face. Pigeon Man jutted his head forward at Guru and began talking rapidly in another language, all clicks and whistles. Gangamma guessed by the look on Ondu's face that he wasn't saying anything nice.

'Guru, eh? It is a fitting name for you, since you teach abomination. Your body is a travesty of its former self!'

'Chitrasena!' said Guru in delight. 'Chitra, Chitra, Chitra! Hello O Chitra! Not ascended yet, huh?'

'No, but I will eventually. You? *Never!*' said Chitra, his red eyes gleaming madly.

'Actually, my teeth are diamond,' said Guru. 'Does that make me part-perfect?'

'So your new name is a mark of wisdom, is it? Pah! Guru!' Chitrasena spat out the word.

'They started calling me Guru at the menagerie in Dwarasamudram.'

'You were in a menagerie?' asked Chitra in horror. 'You let humans *see* you?'

'Yes, they even tried to feed me! I was quite popular with the humans. They thought I was wise,' said Guru cheerfully. In the still air, his voice carried everywhere.

'What are they saying?' said Gangamma to Ondu who whispered a hurried translation. 'I think the gharial is really getting on Pigeon Man's nerves,' she ended.

Gangamma laughed, which meant that all the yakshas turned their attention from Guru on her ear to her face.

She grinned weakly at them. They dismissed her and turned back to Guru.

'Since I'm here, you can let this poor child go home,' said Guru.

'He wants to send me home,' whispered Ondu.

'Good!' whispered back Gangamma.

'No, we can't,' said Chitra. 'Pitiful she might be, but she is now part-yaksha. An abomination! Your friend runs through her. We have to dissolve her.'

'You don't *have* to,' said Guru. 'She's human. They eat all the time. She's much more grains and pulses and brinjal than she is a yaksha. Actually, she's mostly upma, thanks to Gangamma here. There's nothing to be done about it. Dissolve me instead.'

'No!' shouted Chitra, his voice rising to a screech.

Many of the yakshas turned hopefully to a tall woman-shaped figure who stood silently behind Ondu. For a moment she said nothing. Then she moved forward, slowly, and stood facing Gangamma. Her face was calm and she angled it so both Guru and the other yakshas could see her.

'You're a lump of stone and metal,' said Jayanti to Guru, her voice as firm as her bearing. 'You are not wholly diamond, yet your body is still and hard. You have no flesh and do not eat or breathe. You cannot absorb or excrete. You will not grow, you cannot change. I . . . no, *we* will not call for vengeance on you.'

Many other yakshas nodded and murmured. The yakshas moved into little groups, talking in low, serious voices.

'Now what?' whispered Gangamma.

Ondu explained, and added, 'That's Jayanti. She's the chough's sister. His name was Jayant! I never knew.' Gangamma made a sympathetic hmm-ing sound, but Ondu went on, 'I think Jayanti's a bit sorry. It sounds to me like they won't kill the gharial.'

'Why would they?' snapped Gangamma. 'This is the stupidest thing I've ever seen. These people make the gardeners look smart!' she added, hissing her Ss extra violently in annoyance.

'Shhh,' said Jayanti, and the yakshas fell silent. 'We are agreed,' she told Guru. 'You are free to go. You have, in a way, become perfect. You have ascended.'

'He's not perfect! He's an abomination! We are not agreed! I never agreed. This is not just!' said Chitra—his soft cooing voice was harsh and screechy now. 'Nala, tell them!'

'The sabha agrees,' said Treeish. Ondu didn't think the name Nala suited him. 'I do not like it, but Jayanti is right. Justice is done. The human is unimportant. And that Guru, that *ornament*, is no longer one of us. Our part is over.'

'Not yet. The tree still lives,' said Chitra. A winged yaksha walked into the sabha, carrying the remains of the apple tree. As he strode to the centre of the room, he morphed into the leopard yaksha. He sliced at the apple tree's trunk. Clear sap welled up in the wound and spilt out.

'Is that . . .?' whispered Nala. 'What are you . . .?'

Chitrasena waved one wing in a slashing gesture, and a huge bolt of lightning shot through the hole in the roof. For a second, the rest of the sabha was dark against the white-hot bar of lightning that stretched across the room, from the roof to where the apple tree lay on the floor. There was a crack, and the light was gone, leaving only the burnt trunk of the apple tree, split in half. Ondu screamed and fell. A thick, sickly smell of burning filled the sabha. Gangamma was coughing as she knelt over Ondu and saw a red jagged mark at her throat.

'She's burnt too!' she shouted hoarsely.

Nala had caught Chitra's arm and was talking softly and earnestly, trying to calm him down. Jayanti bent over Gangamma and said in a low voice, 'Leave now!'

'How?' asked Gangamma, still on the floor.

'With me!' said the gharial.

'No!' shouted Chitra and more lightning appeared. Small jagged lines of light branched and crackled across the air. Either Chitra was losing control over it, or he wanted to strike everyone in the sabha. A small bolt shot past Gangamma's nose and hit the gharial, who absorbed it. Gangamma felt her head pushed back and her ear hurt.

'Take it off!' said Jayanti.

'No!' said Gangamma.

'Do you know how hot molten gold can get?'

Gangamma's fingers were stiff. She fumbled, and took the gharial off just in time, as a massive bolt struck it, blinding her. Tiny stones clattered to the floor, and hot gold splashed. The floor hissed and melted where the gold touched it.

'No, no, no!' cried Gangamma, blinking furiously. She took off her other earring, a golden bell, and scooped up as much of the gold and stones as she could. Guru was not large, and except where he had melded into the floor she got most of him.

'Let him be or I'll strike lightning through you next!' Chitra hissed at her.

'No! Stop him!' yelled many voices.

Yakshas grabbed Chitra. The egret waved a hand over him, and Chitra turned to stone, his neck feathers still gleaming iridescent.

Gangamma was still scraping half-melted gold off the floor.

As she scrabbled, Jayanti was growing larger and shinier.

'Padmavati! Guha! Make sure they keep talking. No more killing. Don't do anything till I come back. I'll be quick,' shouted Jayanti. A root-limbed yaksha nodded and strode forward briskly.

Jayanti grabbed Gangamma and Ondu.

'What're you doing?' shouted Gangamma.

'The magic will wear off soon. You must be gone when Chitra regains his usual form,' said Jayanti. Huge black wings grew, flapping as they appeared and she flew them out of the hall and into a cold sky. Everything was white, a vast sheet of ice that stretched as far as the eye could see, glittering under a white sun. Gangamma yelped with cold—it nipped at her finger and toes, and her nose went numb. Jayanti flapped her wings, apparently unaffected by the cold. She flew enormously high and fast, and the ice fields gave way to grasslands, forests, mountain ranges, fields and rivers. Gangamma's limbs froze stiff and she could no longer feel them. This was good because they no longer hurt; but she was afraid that if they fell off, she might not notice till it was too late to go back and find them.

Jayanti began to fly lower. The land felt familiar—the hills here were a familiar shade of green, and the air smelt of trees and flowers Gangamma knew. Jayanti slowed, and descended slowly on to a plateau. She placed Gangamma and Ondu gently in a depression in the grass. She half-morphed into a woman and knelt before Gangamma, who lay there feeling too stunned to move.

She gestured to the gold earring that Gangamma was still clutching in one hand. 'I'm sorry about Ashokamitra. You were friends?'

'Guru,' said Gangamma. 'He liked the name.'

Jayanti nodded. 'If Ondu lives . . . tell her the apple tree's yaksha name was Mahendra. Ask her to remember him. And tell her that I will remember her for taking care of my brother. She did her best. I cannot say if she was right about him or I was. But she was . . . she *was* kind. Now I must go back and see that this vengeance ends,' she said. 'You will have to make your way home from here—it's only about half an hour by wing.'

She morphed back into the winged form and leapt towards the sky, her powerful wings beating steadily. Gangamma lay tiredly on the ground and watched her climb higher and higher. She was asleep before Jayanti was out of sight.

Chapter 6

Jayanti didn't want to go back just yet. She didn't know when she'd get another chance to be Outside. It had become clear to her that the sabha needed leaders—leaders who were not Chitrasena and his friends. Leaders who knew about Outside, leaders who thought about everyday things, not just distant dreams of perfection. They needed her—they had looked to her when Chitra had hurled lightning in the sabha. She would lead. At least until she could find someone better. The thought gave Jayanti a certain pride—but she was not yet ready to take on the sabha.

Jayanti flew instead to the mountains where Jayant had lived for so long. She held her wings wide and still and let the air currents carry her through the valley. A couple of choughs flew below, twirling joyfully in the air. Jayanti shrank into a chough too. She flapped her new wings— surprisingly powerful for such small wings—and flew down to join them. She swooped and veered sharply up and then dived down again. She looped around a peak, her small strong wings turning with happy precision. Then, daring, she somersaulted once and then again and again, spinning delightedly.

Then she rose high and morphed into her winged form. She flew fast and straight north. She had Chitra to deal with and a sabha to lead.

Gangamma blinked in the sun. Her ear still hurt. Next to her, Ondu was absolutely still. Gangamma bent over her and murmured, 'Are you all right? Ondu?' but nothing twitched, and Ondu's eyes were blank when Gangamma gently pulled the lids up.

Gangamma stood up with difficulty and surveyed the landscape. She knew they couldn't be far from home, for she had seen her hills from the air, but she didn't know *how* far they were from home. Or where they even were. The landscape around them was hilly, but these hills were skeletal compared to the hills around Giripuram, their rocks jutting out everywhere, with only grasses to pad them. Gangamma walked around a little and finally found water collected in a rocky hollow. She dragged Ondu there and undressed her to see how much damage the lightning had done.

The entire right side of Ondu's body, from her toes to her shoulder, was covered in a delicate network of deep purple-red burns. They branched and twined, as if she had been branded by a tree. The skin around the burns was a paler red, and looked angry and swollen.

Gangamma dipped Ondu's skirt in the water and carefully bathed all the burns. Then she dressed Ondu back in her wet clothes, hoping that keeping her cool would help.

Her legs ached. Her toes and fingers were stiff from sleeping outdoors all night, and her head throbbed from missing her morning coffee. Gangamma tried lifting Ondu a couple of times. The second time, she flopped down next to her and lay down. In a minute she was asleep again.

'Hey!' someone shouted. 'Hey Ajji!'

Gangamma awoke with a start. It was bright noon. A bullock cart stood before her. A man was sitting on it, looking suspiciously at her.

'What are you doing here?' he asked.

'We were going to Giripuram,' she said. 'My granddaughter was struck by lightning.'

'Oh, pilgrims!' said the man, relaxing immediately, as Gangamma had hoped he would, 'I can give you a lift.' He was still abrupt, but he seemed quite kind. He lifted Ondu up and put her gently on top of the hay he was carrying. Then he helped Gangamma climb up in the front with him. He clicked his tongue at the bullocks and off they went.

It was a horrible journey. The man was nice, but he had strong opinions on all kinds of things Gangamma either hadn't heard of (why the cloth woven in some distant land was so expensive) or didn't care about (how to cook some kind of rare sea fish) or both (why the current raja was a blood-sucking louse). Since no king had visited or taxed Giripuram in generations, and pilgrims paid for its roads,

Gangamma was gloriously ignorant and uncaring about taxes and kings.

She nodded and went *hmmm* a lot, falling into strange dark dreams and then waking up with a start to find herself still in the cart and the man still talking.

Gangamma was tired and achey when the bullock cart finally rumbled up to her house. In fact, she was so weary she didn't even glare when the bullocks began nibbling on the jasmine creeper that climbed near her door.

The bullock-cart man helped her carry Ondu into the house and up the stairs. They laid Ondu on her bed. Gangamma took her boots off and put a blanket over her, though it wasn't cold. She dribbled some sugar water into her mouth, but Ondu's mouth was slack and the sugar water fell onto the pillow below her head.

Defeated, Gangamma patted her shoulder and went downstairs to thank the bullocks and their man with an armful of roses and marigold and jasmine.

After they left she waded into the tank, clutching her bell earring, which was now half-solid, its hollow filled with tiny stones and oddly shaped lumps of gold all squished together.

'Guru the gharial, I got as much of you here as I could,' she told it. Her voice was choked and her eyes red and watery. She bent, and buried the earring among the dead lotus stems. 'Be well!' she told it miserably.

The next day, she forced herself to go the market, carrying no lotuses and limping. She felt incredibly old and tired. She told brief, untrue versions of the story to everyone—Ondu was kidnapped by bandits, she went to rescue her, but the child had been struck by lightning, and oh, her blue lotuses had died in the meantime. She kept out all bits about yakshas and gharials, and tree-bonding and gardener gods, and refused to even think about the mysterious sabha. It seemed simpler.

The next week went by in a blur. Gangamma felt numb. Karthik and Renu had tried to be superior and sympathetic about how she was no longer one of them, but she couldn't concentrate on what they were saying long enough to be offended. They soon went away, for there is nothing more dissatisfying than trying to feel superior to someone whose eyes glaze over when you start to speak.

'Arrogant as ever,' Renu could be heard sighing as they walked away.

'You'd think, under the circumstances, she'd be a little more repentant, and a little less snooty. . .' Karthik agreed, his voice fading into the friendly noise of the bazaar.

Most of the other gardeners were kinder. They all felt a little guilty for accusing Ondu of witchcraft and chasing her away. And Gangamma was so miserable that feuding with her would simply not be fun for anyone involved.

One evening, Gangamma was sitting by the tank when Meena came by. 'When are you going to tell someone the real story? We all know something terrible happened,' she said. She said it gruffly, and a bit bossily, but coming from Meena that was almost a hug. Gangamma was so horrified to find she was so touched that she was almost in tears. Luckily she'd had a lot of practice being rude to Meena, and could manage it even—maybe especially—when she was really upset.

'Nonsense!' she said.

But she said it almost affectionately, and Meena left feeling quite kindly towards her.

The next morning, Gangamma woke up to find Bana and Thimma sitting on her doorstep. 'You're not some child of fifty, Gangamma,' said Bana. 'Enough brooding. Tell us what happened.'

Gangamma was so groggy and surprised that she told them everything. She ended with how she only managed to bring back some of Guru's remains.

'Can we see Ondu?' asked Thimma.

Gangamma silently took them up. Bana checked Ondu's wrist for a pulse.

'Nothing,' she said.

She tried her neck and shook her head

'I'm sorry,' said Thimma. 'I can't imagine what we can do for her now.'

They helped Gangamma gather her miserable baskets and walked to the bazaar together. 'You'll feel better if you eat my dosai instead of your awful cooking,' said Thimma. 'I'll make you an extra-crunchy one.'

Gangamma's day went on in a dull haze until suddenly, Bana was standing by her. 'So Ondu is part-tree?' she asked. 'I'm having a hard time imagining a part-tree human. Will flowers grow from her hair? Will they ever become fruit?'

Gangamma looked at her open-mouthed. For she had an idea.

'What?' said Bana.

'She is! I'm the most gormless gardener in the world!' bellowed Gangamma.

All the gardeners looked askance, but Bana didn't care. A slow grin spread across her face.

'Aha!' she shouted.

'Exactly!' said Gangamma. 'She needs soil. Sun. Compost. Maybe even water. Bana, will you watch my flowers?'

'Nonsense,' said Bana. 'Let someone steal them. In fact, I'm leaving my fruit here too. Let's go feed your apprentice!'

So Bana and Gangamma walked home as fast as they could. Bana grabbed a spade and started to dig into the marigold patch. 'How much mud will she need?' she asked, shovelling some into a plate.

'Wait, no. That's not enough. We have to bring Ondu here,' said Gangamma.

'Are you really going to plant a girl in your garden?' asked Bana, simultaneously amused and horrified.

'Not in my garden!' said Gangamma, as if it were obvious. 'I'm planting her in the tank.'

Bana made a snorting sound.

'And I hope it'll only be temporary,' added Gangamma. She didn't think it was funny at all.

They half-dragged, half-carried Ondu down the stairs and into the garden. They put her in Gangamma's wheelbarrow and took her to the edge of the tank, where they put her feet in a large pot and buried them in mud. They packed the pot with soil and compost till her knees.

'What I'm about to do is a rough-and-ready travesty of a sacred lotus-grower ritual,' she told Bana. 'Don't tell anyone.'

'Okay,' shrugged Bana. 'It's not *my* ritual, it's yours.'

'And *I* don't care if I'm doing it wrong,' said Gangamma. 'Now help me lower her in.'

They lowered Ondu and her pot into the tank, among the roots of the blue lotus. Then Gangamma took out a knife and made a small slash on each of Ondu's palms. Blood dripped down and made pale pink swirls in the water.

'The blood's flowing, so her heart is still working,' said Bana. 'Even if it's too slow or too weak for me to tell.'

Gangamma pulled up a handfuls of lotus roots and held them against the blood for a few minutes. These she planted in the pot, at Ondu's feet.

'Done!' said Bana, with a final pat to the soil. They stepped back to look at their newly planted girl. Nothing happened.

'Does she look a little less scorched to you?' asked Gangamma hopefully. Bana shook her head.

'Oh,' said Gangamma sadly. She had been so sure this would work.

'Trees are slow,' said Bana comfortingly. 'Give her time. Let's go back to the bazaar and rescue my fruit.'

In the evening, Gangamma raced back to the tank. She gently picked up Ondu's wrist and felt for a pulse. Nothing. She held it for another two minutes, talking softly. She told Ondu about the bullock-cart man. 'Oh, and the apple tree's name was Mahendra,' she ended. Still nothing. 'I'll go then. I'll come back to see you in the morning,' she said sadly.

She tucked a bit of Ondu's hair behind her ears and then it happened—she felt a tiny flutter on her neck. Ondu was alive! Or at least, Gangamma corrected herself, not yet dead. She sat down on the tank steps and sure enough, five minutes later, Ondu's throat pulsed again, slowly, and just once.

Gangamma ate her dinner there that night, feeling suddenly lighter and more herself than she had been in weeks. A light breeze blew off the tank, laden with its usual smell of pine and cinnamon and . . . 'Oh!' said Gangamma. No wonder she was feeling happier. She waded back into the pond and peered at Ondu's pot. A lotus was blooming. The other lotuses in the tank had put forth leaves and buds too—it was as if they had never died.

'Bloodthirsty slime!' Gangamma said happily to them, sniffing deeply.

The End

Three days later, Gangamma woke up to the sweetish smell of batter turning crunchy. She walked to the kitchen and found Ondu at the stove, making dosai.

A large daft grin spread across her face. 'You're well!' she said.

Ondu grinned back, her old toothy grin. 'I feel wonderful. Your compost really is the best,' she said. And they both laughed madly till they started hiccupping.

When the dosais were done, Gangamma made strong coffee. Ondu had scraped a coconut and was now topping it with a generous spoonful of spluttering mustard seeds to make a truly delicious-smelling chutney. They took their plates and tumblers out and sat on the steps to the tank. The blue lotuses were in full bloom and a delicate scent wafted around. Gangamma wondered idly if she should put cinnamon in her coffee.

'Do you think the rest of the twelve are around somewhere?' asked Ondu.

'Probably,' said Gangamma. 'We should go to the temple courtyard one day and figure out exactly what they look like.'

'So we can avoid them?' laughed Ondu.

'Exactly!' said Gangamma.

'Um,' said Ondu, in a hesitant half-cough. She stood up straight, and her face was still and determined. Gangamma wondered how she could ever have thought of her as twelve years old.

'What?' Gangamma replied as encouragingly as she could.

'I wanted to tell you . . . my real name, the one my parents gave me—it's Karpuravalli.'

'That's not bad,' said Gangamma judicially. 'A herb's not as good as a flower, I'd agree—but decent. Quite an attractive little plant. Nice smell.'

'Is it?' said Ondu. 'Oh!'

'No, nothing to be ashamed of there,' said Gangamma kindly.

Ondu laughed then, loud and clear. 'My mother said she was a princess from some play she had once seen, you know. She said it was romantic. I hated the name!'

'Not a play I've seen,' said Gangamma—not that she had seen too many. 'No shame in introducing yourself to people as Karpuravalli. Even Meena can't say too much against it. It's . . . respectable.'

Ondu grinned. 'But is it respectable enough for an apprentice?'

'You're a thousand, three hundred and eleven years old. And might be part yaksha now,' said Gangamma. 'Or a tree.

Maybe even both. I think we can agree that you're a bit experienced to be anyone's apprentice.'

'I was hoping you'd take me to the bazaar and teach me the fine art of bargaining,' said Ondu.

'Hmm. You can be an assistant with an option of becoming a partner in a year,' said Gangamma. 'I'll put you in charge of the wild flowers. I've been thinking we can grow them in little pots and sell them like that—if they're never picked, they'll last longer. We can do what Bana does with her fruit, and sell different ones every few weeks. If you'd like to, of course.'

'I *would* like to,' said Ondu.

'Then you won't mind if I leave you in charge every now and then so I can travel? I've only been on three holidays—one was when I came to your mountain and stole your tree, the second was running away and only lasted a few hours, and the third was when I went to a desert and then a moon of Jupiter to avoid people, and I was miserable right through. I'd like to go on a proper holiday, see the mountains.'

'But the gharial is gone. How will you go?' asked Ondu.

'I'll walk,' laughed Gangamma. 'As you did a thousand years ago. And since no one is chasing me, I can go as slowly as I want. Maybe I'll collect us some wild flowers too.'

'No flowers—I don't want a bag of dead flowers. Get us something we can keep and grow,' said Ondu. 'But I'm *not* saying you should steal any more trees . . .' she added sternly.

'Is it stealing if I collect seeds? Maybe some cuttings?' said Gangamma.

'Get us some nice bulbs?' said Ondu. 'I've heard that's less criminal than stealing an entire tree.'

They cackled delightedly together, and then sat down to make a list of things for Gangamma to take with her on her travels.

And that's how the Giripuram bazaar became famous for its wild flowers. It is said that even today, if a stranger comes anywhere near the town and tries to pick a flower—any flower—a girl in a long blue sweater, a pink skirt and bright blue boots comes by and shouts, 'Shove off!'

Acknowledgements

I owe massive debts of gratitude to—Appa, Amma, Tulch, and KK for criticism, puns, animal trivia, character names, random nit-picking, and everything else; my grandmothers for introducing me to all kinds of mythology, folklore and other good stuff; Nandini, Roh and Gankhu for wading through many drafts, and always knowing what doesn't work and why; Shikha for knowing all about apple trees; Smed and Wopse for long walks, excellent company, and even some truly hideous barking; the always lovely nurseries of Siddapura; Archana for early encouragement and making everything look fantastic; Niyati for careful and fine-toothed copy-editing; and Nimmy, who began this, carrot-and-sticked me into writing it on schedule, and then edited it into respectability.

Read More in Puffin

The Assassin Nuns of Pistachio
Manisha Anand

Nuns with Guns!

When eleven-year-old Ann is sent to live with the famous Assassin Nuns of Pistachio, she expects nothing less than a life of swashbuckling adventures and covert rescue missions. Instead, she meets a group of mild-mannered women who prefer soufflés to sword fighting and haven't stepped out of their mountaintop abbey in years.

After Ann discovers that there's something very nasty going on in Pistachio, she decides it's time the nuns lived up to their reputation. Armed with wooden spoons, gardening gloves and a malfunctioning robot broom, can these unlikely heroes save the day?

Read More in Puffin

Red Kite Adventure
Leela Gour Broome

'Identical!'

At a chance meeting that might've been fated all along, two twelve-year-olds, Veer and Arzaan, are stunned by their resemblance to each other!

As they exchange stories, their friendship rapidly deepens over pooping messenger pigeons that one can call with a special whistle, and Dada's kites dancing in the wind with colourful tails. But their joyous days come to an abrupt halt when Veer is kidnapped and Arzaan makes a fatal sacrifice to rescue his friend.

Will their bond be enough to save them both or is there only so much two young boys can do?

A gripping escapade and a heart-warming friendship make *Red Kite Adventure* an extraordinary tale that is sure to enthral young readers.